DAVID LE COURAGEUX

Undercover Legends

The Real Mr and Mrs Smith

HENDRY
PUBLISHING
www.hendrypublishing.com

First edition

ISBN: 978-1-7398136-6-6

Cover art by 100 Covers
Editing by Sheryl Lee

This book was professionally typeset on Reedsy.
Find out more at reedsy.com

"People trust their eyes above all else - but most people see what they wish to see, or what they believe they should see; not what is really there."

—Zoë Marriott, Shadows on the Moon

Contents

Foreword

Dragnet was an American radio, television and motion-picture series, enacting the cases of a dedicated Los Angeles police detective, Sergeant Joe Friday and his partners. The show took its name from the police term "dragnet", meaning a system of coordinated measures for apprehending criminals or suspects.

One of *Dragnet's* trademarks was the show's opening narration: "Ladies and gentlemen: the story you are about to hear is true. Only the names have been changed to protect the innocent." This underwent minor revisions over time. The "only" and "ladies and gentlemen" were dropped at some point and for the television version "hear" was changed to "see."

The series was first aired on television in 1951 then revived in 1967.

In the case of this novel: Ladies and gentlemen: the story you are about to read is true. Only the names and some locations have been changed to protect the innocent, and the not-so-innocent.

The author asks you to think of this novel as a modern form of "dragnet", meaning a system of coordinated measures for apprehending criminals or suspects, in that undercover police officers are part of that system. Dominic and Samantha Smith are undercover police officers, and this is their story.

Why Undercover Legends?

A legend is an undercover officer's false persona or identity. They may use several of these legends for different deployments. Dominic and Samantha Smith never considered themselves to be legends in the murky world of covert policing. So, it's a play on words.

Jack Reacher

At a Bouchercon some years ago, Lee Child was part of a panel on characters in thrillers. An audience member asked him a question about character change. "Every character has to have an arc, right?"

"Why?" Child said. "There doesn't have to be character change. We don't need no stinkin' arcs."

Everybody in the room cracked up. Child went on to explain that he loves Dom Perignon champagne, and he wants it to taste the same each time. And so, too, he wants his Jack Reacher books to offer the same pleasurable experience every time out. Reacher doesn't change. Reacher does his thing. It's how he does it that provides the pleasure.

That's how we see the Dominic and Samantha Smith characters. They don't need no stinkin' character arc. They are who they are and do what they do, and we hope you agree their tales make for fascinating storytelling.

But... allow us to let you into a not very secret secret. If you really want to know what makes Dom and Sam tick, download the book *Meet Mr and Mrs Smith*. Did we mention it's free to subscribers to the Undercover Legends mailing list and to anyone who has purchased this book? Please see the back of the book for details of where and how to download it. You will also learn why we and us is used by the author instead of I/me.

Operation Candle, Book Two in the Undercover Legends series, will soon be available to purchase at a special pre-order price

Acknowledgement

Thanks and much gratitude are extended to Sheryl Lee for her editing skills, Stephen Bentley's VIP Team for beta reading and other valuable feedback, and to the design team at 100 Covers for the covers for all books in the Undercover Legends series. Yes, there are more on the way.

Prologue

"It's written in the stars," someone, somewhere once said. Dominic and Samantha Smith became two comets in the undercover universe. For many years, they burned brightly, separately carving out successful careers as elite undercover cops until they collided. And, what a collision! Rather than be destroyed in the inferno, eventually they fused into a fearsome partnership within a formidable undercover deployment known as Operation Candle.

Together, Dom and Sam became stronger. Both would scoff at any notion they were romantics, but their story is a romance even if it was partly born out of pragmatism. They became partners in life as well as undercover partners. They also became the guardians of an extended family that included Sam's son, James, and Dom's children from his two previous marriages, H and BB from his second marriage, and Jane and Lesley from his first marriage. Dom always had a close and supportive relationship with all four of his children. They grew up as brothers and sisters minus the prefix 'step.'

James also became part of the Smith family as did his birth father, Ken, in a way. Sam and Ken were divorced amicably after a few years of marriage when they were still young. Sam knew it happened because she was determined to succeed in her career as a police officer. She was another statistic in the high divorce rate amongst career police officers, particularly detectives. Now divorced, she was resolved to forge ahead in her police career as a single mum. That wasn't easy as misogyny was common in the police service. With the help of Ken and her parents, Sam was able to arrange childcare to pursue her goals in a demanding environment.

Sam checked off those goals. First, she was a CID detective. Then she worked on major crime investigation units until she decided she wanted to become an undercover police officer, a UCO. At first, her line manager tried to tell her she wouldn't make it as she was a single mother. Undeterred and in typical Sam-style, she bypassed this misogynist's nonsense and went straight to the very top – the Assistant Chief Constable (Crime) in her force. He approved her application and eventually she got there after passing the tough National Undercover Accreditation Course (NUTAC) some years after Dom had taken a similar career path. Their stars were now aligned but their trajectories didn't cross until Dom needed a female UCO for Operation Candle.

At the early stages of Operation Candle, and whilst Dom was putting together his team, he heard about Sam's role in the money laundering operation. She had made her mark in the world of elite undercover policing.

Chapter 1: Money Laundering

The deployment on the money laundering job brought Sam to the attention of those who matter in the world of undercover policing. In time, she would also come to Dom's attention when he recruited her for his Operation Candle team. Life as a police officer wasn't always that straightforward for her. Sam had been a police cadet, then at nineteen became a regular copper. At twenty, she became pregnant with James and married his father, Ken. On returning to work Sam concentrated on her career, rapidly progressing to the CID as a detective. That focus cost her marriage, for when she was twenty-three Ken and Sam amicably separated. Ken later remarried but he and his new wife were still part of an extended family for James as they provided childcare when Sam's mum and dad were not available.

Sam, now a single mum, progressed from regular CID work to becoming a Test Purchase Officer, a TPO, involved in street-level drugs buys. This was a steppingstone to undercover work once she had successfully passed the National Undercover Training Accreditation Course, NUTAC. By the time she gave evidence in the money laundering trial, Sam was the real deal: an elite undercover police officer.

Every inch of her svelte five feet-nine inches, looking like a wealthy and successful Independent Financial Advisor, an IFA, Sam walked into the number one court at the Old Bailey from a door behind the judge's bench. Well, why wouldn't she? Unlike a real IFA, she had not spent years gaining her spurs and sitting exams, she'd done a crash course to learn her commodity... money and how to launder it. That's what elite undercover officers do. Settling into the witness box behind a screen shielding her from the public and press, Sam turned to the judge, the Recorder of London and gave him an almost indiscernible nod of respect. Those in the know may have noticed a subtle nod from the judge. Then the bailiff approached and asked her if she wished to affirm or swear on the bible. Before she answered, Sam glanced across at the twelve men and women who made up the jury. She was ready, a little nervous as always, but confident she had performed her undercover role within the rules of evidence and the rule of law.

Was it almost two years ago? Sam's thoughts drifted off to an earlier time.

Raking through designer clothing in one of the many shops at Bicester Outlet Village, her phone rang. Sam was still thinking about earlier that day and her evidence at Oxford Crown Court over a job to do with a firm of armed robbers. She had rented a lock-up next to them to infiltrate, befriend, monitor, and inform on them. The robbers were good company to be around, but they were robbers, and she was an undercover cop. *Sorry boys, I guess I won't be getting a Christmas card this year, unlike last year,* Sam thought. It was JW, her cover officer, on the phone. *Do I let it go to answer phone or take it? My time at this precise moment is focused on clothing, not you, JW. Leave a message, I'll listen to it between shops.*

That's what she did. 'You have one new message, today at two twenty-one' her voicemail announced.

"Hi, Sam. If I was a betting man, right now I'll wager you are shopping in that designer outlet near Oxford. I got your message to say you have been released from court, thanks. Did their cover team look after you all right? When you get a minute give me a bell, nothing urgent, tomorrow will do when you are driving back home. Have a good night tonight with the op team. Cheers, stay safe mate."

'To listen to the message again press...' Sam didn't need to hear that automated voice anymore. She often thought it was like having two husbands with JW as her cover officer. He knew her almost as well as Ken used to, her ex. Sam believed he could even read her mood when she walked into the office and used this skill to his full advantage.

The drive home was okay. Sam only encountered a couple of blokes who thought their cars were an extension of their penises. *Tossers*, she thought. She called JW and arranged to meet in town at their favourite café after she had visited the gym and worked off the curry and bubbles from the night out with the op team. Sam always took her red gym bag with her; it was part of her deployment gear.

"What do you know about money laundering, Sam?" JW asked. "I know your old man used to be in the game, did you pick any bits and pieces up from him?"

Sam thought for a few seconds. "What? Ken's a washer of money? He's my ex, you should know better than calling him my old man."

"I'll rephrase," JW said. "Your ex, he's in finance, right?"

"I'm kidding, I know some of the language they use, words and phrases. I heard enough from Ken. What's this all about, what are we looking at, JW?" she asked raising her coffee cup to her lips and looking over the brim of the cup into his dark brown eyes.

JW put his cup down and took a deep breath. "I have been involved in a couple of meetings over the last few weeks with the boss about an international, multi-agency bit of work that they are trying to put together. One of the tactics they are looking at is an undercover deployment into the subjects. Nothing has been agreed yet. The commodity is money. Money laundering to be precise. It involves a core nominal who seems to pay tax on an income of twenty-three thousand pounds a year and lives in a small flat in South London. That's all bollocks. In short, he is washing his money from bent sales of properties, villas, apartments and complexes in Spain, Portugal, and the Canaries. The red flashing light for us, and I mean red light is the killing of the nominal's money man. He was shot dead outside a restaurant on the Costa del Sol. Professional hit, two guys on a motorbike, two shots in the head.

"The Spanish old bill, National Police Corps, the CNP, aren't knocking themselves out investigating. Just another dead dodgy Brit as far as they are concerned. MI6 have an input as do MI5, Customs, Serious Fraud Office, City of London Police, National Crime Squad, Uncle Tom Cobley and all. I don't think it's a runner to be honest, Sam, but if it is an option on the table, I want us to be ahead and waiting with a game plan up our sleeve, ready to go."

Sam had experienced numerous discussions over the years with bosses, other UCOs and cover officers about 'possible jobs' and they never materialised, and that's what she thought about this one. She had a phrase 'Too many moving parts' and this had too many. "Well, sweetie, what is it you are saying to me? Why are you here right now talking about a job you don't think will happen?" Sam was trying not to sound disappointed at the suggestion that JW thought it was a nonrunner.

JW continued explaining his thoughts. "I just wanted to put it on your radar, Sam, and ask you to have a think and perhaps take a bit of time researching the role and what you would need to know to carry it off. You certainly look the part; you could walk the walk and talk the talk. You could have a chat with your ex, pick his brains. You know what to do. Give it some thought, you've got some down time now, you might as well fill it with something. What do you say?"

And that was about two years ago. Because of Ken, Sam had some knowledge of IFAs, so that was a start. 'Know your commodity' was a piece of advice she was given as a UCO and that applied to everything: drugs, guns, fags, booze, and money. So, with her inner dogged determination she set about learning how to be an IFA. Sam initially went to Ken. He knew her job and didn't ask the bleeding obvious. She also knew a couple of mates from the gym. Sue had her own company and was a fully qualified IFA and Stewart had worked in overseas investments and knew the system inside out. The problem with Sue and Stewart was they thought Sam worked for the Civil Service as a National Training Officer; hence the reason she was on the missing list from time to time. Sam hated telling lies to friends, but with what she did for a living, needs must sometimes. Sam came up with a cover story about a training course she was putting together about money laundering and needed to understand the subject better.

She invited them both to a coffee in the lounge bar at the gym after a workout so she could pick their brains. Stewart volunteered to speak on the course in relation to international legislation and Sue wanted to come along for the ride and a few drinks in the bar in the evenings. After a couple of weeks of researching Google, grilling Ken, and pumping Sue and Stewart for information, she was almost satisfied with her commodity knowledge if she ever needed to use it.

That's the thing: almost is not good enough. And she told JW as much. He came up trumps and put her in touch with Rosie Horgan, an assets recovery expert with the Regional Crime Squad. She was used to untangling a web of false money trails involving shell companies and offshore banking. Sam and Rosie became good friends. So much so, Rosie's tutorials took place at Sam's home with the bonus that Rosie turned out to be a first class cook specialising in Italian peasant dishes. And if push came to shove, Rosie didn't mind the odd bit of babysitting if Sam's mum or Ken weren't available.

So, back to today, the Old Bailey, number one court, and all the jurors' eyes fixed on Sam. What did they see and what did they think? They saw a mature woman, attractive, physically fit, blonde hair in a sophisticated 'up style', clear painted nails and light make-up, in a two-piece dark navy suit. They saw a professional businesswoman. Sam often thought about what went through their minds when they heard what she did, how she conducted herself when it got tense and dangerous. She could almost hear their minds ticking – She looks like the woman who lives across the street. She was that person who lives across the street for some of the time. But at other times, she was Detective Constable Samantha Smith, undercover police officer.

The defendants were sitting in the dock on the opposite side of the court room from her as Sam was about to give her evidence in chief. They were Andrew James Cooper, known to her as Andy or Coops, and Sergio Lopez, aka 'The Spaniard.'

Sam took the Bible and card from the bailiff. Holding the Bible high in her right hand, she glanced at the words on the card, but didn't need to read them. Sam recited the oath from memory in a strong, confident manner, just like on the many previous occasions. As the bailiff retrieved the Bible and card, she deliberately looked at Coops and the Spaniard. It was only for a second or two, but enough so she could see and sense the betrayal and hate in their eyes. Sam stared back to show her lack of fear or intimidation.

Coops could have avoided his day in court, well, three weeks in court as it turned out. He should have listened to Mr Terrence Walker, his private investigator, the PI. Sam could honestly say without fear of contradiction it was one of the most challenging and frightening times she had faced as a UCO. Not just the car chase but having to confront Coops knowing what they both knew. During that meeting, they were in a high-stake poker game. Both were cheating but Sam had to keep her game face on and try to bluff her way through.

Chapter 2: Paint a Picture

This money laundering operation involved Europol and was being managed by the desk in London. The funding was no problem as the UK had the lead, but the other supporting agencies had deep pockets. The operational team's end game was to recover all expenses and assets under the Proceeds of Crime Act (POCA). Sam had to give Coops and the Spaniard the impression that she was as bent as they were without shouting it from the roof tops. She planned to paint a picture, let them see what they wanted to see and let them walk into it. "

All her contact with the Spaniard was recorded, whether over the phone or a face-to-face meeting. At Sam's first meeting with the Spaniard, she told him she wanted to pay cash for the apartment. "Euros, sterling or dollars, whatever you are happy with."

He didn't appear fazed by the proposal. "Okay. An unusual method but not a deal breaker," he said.

"I'm finally getting shot of my other half and I need to spend some cash that's sloshing around. Is that okay with you?"

Without looking up from the paperwork on the sales desk in front of him, he said, "As I say, senora, it's not a deal breaker, but we will do things slightly differently to smooth the path.

Euros are perfectly acceptable if we can agree terms." Terms were agreed.

About a year after this first meeting, Sam arrived at Heathrow Terminal Five, or as everyone calls it, T5, after one of her many flights to and from the Iberia Coast. She had been out on one of her meetings with Coops and the Spaniard. The idea was to purchase her third apartment for cash in as many months. The Spaniard told Sam that his boss, Mr Cooper, was in town and would like to buy her dinner. Previously, she had spoken to Coops briefly on recorded phone calls on a couple of occasions. Sam had created an impression by leaving a trail of breadcrumbs during these calls. They, and her business transactions with Senor Sergio Lopez, had achieved their goal. She had managed to get on Mr Cooper's radar as a person of interest. This would be the first time Sam had met him in person. "He's on the hook," she told JW. Plans were made for Sam to meet Cooper on her next trip to Spain.

Sam made her own reservation at the Five Star Puente Romano Beach Resort, Marbella, for a three-day, two-night deployment. She used the same hotel on every visit to build up a legend with the hotel staff and the local restaurants and bars. JW was tucked up in a less swanky two star in the town centre. "Rub of the green, sweetie," she said as they were booking accommodation from the safety and comfort of their office.

They had a dedicated point of contact, via the desk in London, with the Spanish police and their undercover unit. As a tactic and safety measure to avoid unwanted attention from some guy who might fancy his chances with the 'posh, wealthy blonde,' JW obtained the services of a male Spanish UCO to act as Sam's 'fella from Marbella.' Hugo was real eye candy, ten years Sam's junior, tall, dark, and handsome, lean and fit. He could speak Spanish, Portuguese, French and English in a 'to die for' accent. This was not how she described Hugo to Ken, even though he was her ex. In his world, Hugo was in his late fifties, short grey hair, ruddy pitted complexion, and overweight. Another example of need to know, and Ken didn't need to know! Hugo and Sam had got a story ready to run out about their relationship should anyone ask the question. JW and Sam would pull Hugo out of his box on each deployment to enhance her legend and give her an additional reason for visiting Spain. He made Sam look real. JW needed a cover story which was far less attractive than Sam's. He worked for a UK publishing company specialising in travel and tourist guides. A senior member of the operational team always accompanied them on these deployments. They needed some 'real police' with them if the wheels came off. As well as going on the piss with their Spanish counterparts, they did all the handshaking and politics around the job.

Under the international agreement, every deployment had to be notified and approved by the host nation. The high-level mechanics of the operation were way above JW and Sam's pay grades, so they didn't get bogged down with the politics. However, the protocols did have the effect of slowing the job down and was something she had to take into consideration every time she deployed and planned for any future meetings with Coops and Sergio.

Sam made her way by taxi from the airport to her Marbella hotel. JW had travelled the day before to avoid travelling on the same plane. You never know who is examining a flight manifest looking for patterns. He would mix and match his travel day but would always be in country before Sam. He also broke the pattern by sending another cover officer on the odd occasion, but overall, JW was Sam's man.

Sam had booked a table for two, for her and Mr Cooper, in a small traditional restaurant, Casa Perejila, in the hills above Marbella. Hugo and Sam had used the restaurant on a few occasions during the operation and on her visits to Marbella on the build up to enhance their legend. Sam was known to Sofia and Lucas, the owners. Daniel, the head waiter, also knew her. She had arranged to meet Coops in her hotel reception and then travel to the restaurant by taxi. Right on time, Sam saw Sergio walk in with another man. She rightly assumed this to be Mr Andrew Cooper. Sam activated her recording device and stood up as they approached. She stretched out her right hand and offered it to the stranger. "Mr Andrew Cooper, I assume?"

The stranger reached for her hand and gently guided it towards his lips, landing a light kiss like one of those old Cary Grant Hollywood films. "At your service, senora, it is a pleasure to finally meet you, Sam."

Coyly, Sam slightly lowered her head. "The pleasure is all mine, Andrew."

"Please call me Coops. All my friends call me Coops." He released her hand and she extended it towards Sergio.

"Hi, Sergio, I didn't realise you would be coming. Let me call the restaurant and have them lay an additional..."

Before Sam could finish, he cut across her. "No, no, I have only come to drop off Coops, I have a dinner appointment of my own this evening, thank you. So, buenas noches, senora y senor." With that, Sergio left.

Sam told Coops her restaurant plan and that she had to arrange a taxi. "Excellent, Sam, I could eat a horse, I'm starving."

She smiled at him. "I don't believe Sophia and Lucas have horse on the menu, Coops."

Coops was the perfect gent. He held the taxi door open for Sam outside the hotel reception and on arrival at the restaurant.

Daniel opened the restaurant entrance door and smiled on seeing her. "Senora Sam, how lovely to see you again. No Hugo this evening, who is this lucky man? Good evening, senor?" Coops and Daniel shook hands as they introduced themselves to each other.

The restaurant was very popular with locals and was quite busy. Daniel showed them to Sam's go to table in the window where she was able to view people approaching on the pavement and had an overview of the whole restaurant. Sam had been earlier briefed by the boss and JW that the meeting in the restaurant would be covered by a couple of Spanish old bill who would smudge evidence of the meeting, police parlance for obtaining evidence by way of photographs, possibly video, of the meetings between the target or targets and the undercover officers. Any images of the undercover officers would be pixelated out prior to any advance disclosure at the legal process stage.

Sam controlled the conversation over dinner. She made herself look 'criminally attractive' to Coops without really going into too much depth. She added further touches, hinting that he and Sergio might become interested. Sam wanted him to sense she had an edge to her – she wasn't a straight runner. Sam made it clear she was skilled in managing funds in offshore accounts and knew the difference between tax avoidance and tax evasion.

Sam had been briefed to introduce an accountant, Clifford, into the conversation if it felt right. It did feel right. "You need as many layers as possible between you and the audit trail when working with cash, Coops." Sam told him that Clifford had two weaknesses. One, greed. He could never have enough money, which was because of his second weakness: he was a gambler, a big gambler and he wasn't good at it. He owed money to some unsavoury individuals he was servicing and keeping his head just above the waterline.

For his part, Coops didn't disclose much about any of his criminal activity and Sam didn't expect him to. This was him sounding her out. He spoke about his wealth and property portfolio and made a matter of fact mention of the shooting of a friend of his in the past year, emphasizing he avoided unsavoury characters at all costs. "Because you're in the property game over here everyone automatically assumes you're a gangster," he stressed. Taking a breath, he continued, "Who is Hugo?"

Sam was surprised he'd taken over an hour to bring the subject up. "He's my fella in Marbella, darling. He's my self-indulgence. My friend with added benefits as they say. He lives here in Marbella, and we spend time together when I'm out here. After years of a dull boring, lifeless relationship with a cheating shit I'm now enjoying myself, and my toy boy is called Hugo." *That should shut a few doors and is also based on some truth, except my ex wasn't a cheat*, she thought as her mind flashed to her private life.

"Aah, I see, a toy boy, good on you. I see there is a lot to learn about you, my lovely."

She leaned across the table and whispered, "There's lots you don't know about me, sweetie. For now." They finished dinner with a Carajillo coffee while waiting for the taxi which dropped Sam at her hotel.

As she was getting out, Coops said he would get Sergio to give her a ride to the airport the next day. "What time's your flight?"

"Around midday, get him to pick me up at ten. Thanks." The cab pulled away and took Coops to wherever he was staying. Walking away from the cab, Sam made a point of looking at her watch and reading the time and date out aloud before deactivating her recorder. She thought that she should have declined the offer of a ride to the airport, but it seemed the natural thing to do.

Chapter 3: Blonde Bimbo

Sam's flight landed at T5 on time and after the normal customs and producing her covert passport at passport control, she made her way to the long stay car park and jumping into her BMW headed off to the debrief at a hotel about an hour away. She still had her operational head on and knew she had to make sure she was clean, not followed, as she left the airport and before arriving at the debrief location. On descending the spiral ramp of the car park to the exit barriers, Sam was conscious of the three vehicles in convoy following her down the ramp. Nothing unusual with that, but she made a mental note of the colours and make. Black Audi with privacy glass. Red Ford, female driver, and a black Lexus. Sam stopped at the barrier and fumbled in her handbag for the parking ticket as a stalling tactic.

The red Ford went to the barrier to her left, the driver popped in her ticket, the barrier went up and she drove off. The Audi and the Lexus waited behind Sam. She thought, Why not go to the other barrier? The Audi was blocked from changing lanes as he had stopped too close to the back of her Beemer. The Lexus had done the same to the Audi. Why hasn't the Lexus taken up the free lane? Sam took out her ticket, then put it into the machine. The barrier went up and she pulled off slowly. Out came the Audi and overtook her. The driver looked across at Sam as he went by as if to say, 'Blonde bimbo,' I don't think so, sweetie. No sign of the Lexus. She gained speed on the stretch of road towards the M25 motorway, checking the mirrors every ten seconds.

As part of her undercover cop training, Sam attended various courses. She was proficient at handling guns and ammunition. She could test drugs to ensure she wasn't buying crap gear. She could talk round profit margins on various types of merchandise. She could even fit into a contract killing job if she didn't have to do the killing. But one of the best courses was fast, anti, and counter surveillance, evasion/extraction, and defensive driving. Sam was an advanced police driver, which meant she could drive powerful, fast cars safely at high speed, although others wouldn't agree with that.

Sam saw a black car in the rear-view mirror. It could be the Lexus, too far back to be sure and three cars between them. Might be nothing but let's keep an eye on it. Let's do a bit of anti-surveillance to be sure. This technique identified sources of unwanted attention such as the black Lexus. The other technique was counter surveillance, carried out to confirm surveillance is being conducted against you. First, increase speed and change lanes. The Lexus mirrored Sam. It maintained the same distance behind her, using other vehicles to shield him from her view. Sam manoeuvred back into lane one and reduced speed to sixty mph. The Lexus remained the same distance behind her but had no other vehicles for cover. Sam learned two lessons already in this short journey. One, she was under surveillance and two, whoever was in the Lexus was not very good at the job. When you are trained and experienced in surveillance you know what it looks like. Doing surveillance with one car is a non-starter. If you're going to do a job, do it proper. Let's give this muppet in the Lexus a lesson.

Sam floored the pedal and cut across lane two and into lane three. There was plenty more power still under the bonnet of the Beemer. She watched the speedo hit ninety-five and then one hundred. The Lexus came with her. She slowed down slightly to exit the M25 and on to the M3. Although this wasn't her route to the debrief, Sam was aware of the fifty mile an hour speed limit covered by speed cameras on the first part of the M3. Going through that stretch of motorway at ninety miles per hour would capture her registration and that of the Lexus. So, if she failed to get the number, the traffic office would capture it.

Sam called JW and spoke rapidly, "Listen, mate, I've got someone in a black Lexus chasing me. It picked me up at the airport and has stayed with me since, despite my counter/anti-surveillance. We have just pinged the speed cameras at the top of the M3. It will have captured the index. I'm going to exit the M3 at junction four and drive towards Aldershot, loads of ANPR cameras. Mate, get onto the ANPR office and find out who this muppet is. I'll try to shake it off in a built-up area. As far as I can tell it's on its own. I'll keep this phone open and give you a commentary on where I am."

Sam was prioritising what to do. Not a lot of time to think about options, it was a case of fast driving, fast thinking, and fast reactions. She stayed in lane three as she passed the first countdown markers for junction four. Mirrors, check speed and then manoeuvre across lanes two and one, just making the exit slip before the white hatchings. Hard on the brakes as the roundabout loomed in front of her. The Beemer's ABS activated, then she dropped two gears to negotiate the roundabout and take the first exit towards Aldershot. Just as she pulled the steering wheel to the left, Sam caught a view of the Lexus crossing her mirrors from right to left behind her. It seemed the driver was having a problem controlling the car. "JW, I'm on the A331 towards Aldershot, it's still with me." Sam thought, What interest has my pursuer got in me. No time to think about that right now. Whoever it is, why are they determined to let me know he or she wants me?

Sam activated another speed camera on the A331, one of the more traditional cameras that gives a flash when activated. She saw the flash and seconds later a second flash. Traffic was now building up, so she cut down on speed. The Lexus was three or four cars behind. Sam approached a set of traffic lights that had changed to red. Stopping in pole position, she watched the traffic build up behind and in lane two. She could see that the Lexus was trapped by other traffic. Seeing a gap coming up in the traffic crossing in front of her, Sam held the Beemer on the clutch as she built up the engine revs. Releasing the clutch and flooring the accelerator pedal, the Beemer filled the gap as it lunged forward. She pulled the steering wheel to the left, leaving a cacophony of blaring horns and flashing headlights in her slipstream. She ignored all that as she took the first left and sped away. Sam got out of the immediate area as fast and as safely as possible. She knew whoever it was would likely be still searching for her. "You still there, JW?"

"Yes, Sam, sounds like things have settled down. Are you all right, mate?"

"Yeah, thanks darling, I'm running a reverse on a parallel route back to the motorway. All being well I will be with you in the hour." Switching into sarcasm mode, she added, "Give my apologies to the boss for running late." JW chuckled and killed the call.

Chapter 4: ANPR

B y the time she arrived at the debrief her heart rate had returned to her normal of fifty beats per minute and she had regained composure. The team had been double busy working with ANPR, the Automatic Number Plate Recognition office, to identify the Lexus. It was registered to a security company in Hertfordshire. Further company searches showed Private Investigator as the nature of the business with one sole director, Terrance Walker, who had been identified as an associate of Andrew Cooper, the main subject of the operation.

"Guess what, Sam?" JW asked.

Sam didn't hesitate. "Don't tell me. It was nicked from Heathrow today, while he was there meeting a client or some old tosh like that."

JW, with a stupid smile on his face, responded with one word. "Correct."

Right up until the car chase the deployment and dinner with Mr Andrew Cooper had gone well. But this incident gave the team a massive issue around officer safety. For sure his mate Terrance Walker would report back on the car chase. In turn, Coops would expect Sam to mention it to him without him breathing a word. How best to deal with it, was the question? After all, Sam had been out of the country on business concerning the two of them, Coops and her. How, when and where I mention it are the real questions. Not mentioning it was not an option, Sam knew.

The operational team head, the ultimate decision maker, JW and Sam got started on a plan. After a few cups of coffee and kicking around ideas they settled on Sam pulling Coops into a meeting in a public place such as a hotel lounge or restaurant, somewhere they could populate with a cover team to react if it turned nasty. Sam was to tell him about the Lexus car chase and say she had no idea why anyone would have an interest in her. Let's see how he reacts to that. There were a few details to settle but they had a plan. The most difficult part in it for Sam was not revealing she knew that Coops and the driver of the Lexus were associates and that Coops already knew about the car chase. Her attitude, body language or conversations could not give away any of that. Sam was nervous and uneasy about the impending meeting. She was scared.

As they were about to leave the hotel room the boss's phone rang. Sam heard him say, "Yes, Carol, what can I do for you?" He listened in silence for well over a minute, then, "Thanks, Carol, you did the right thing, cheers." He turned to them saying, "Get the kettle on, JW, we've got a problem."

Sam didn't need telling there was a phone tap on Coops' phones and the little room, officially the listening room, had contacted one of the readers, police officers nominated and authorised to read the transcripts of intercepted calls, with some urgent information concerning officer safety. That officer was Sam. The boss began, "Walker has been on the phone to Coops and told him about the car chase. Walker has put into Coops' head that the way you drove suggests you have had training like a police officer would have received. Coops asked if Walker had found where you went from the airport. He, Walker, said you lost him around Aldershot in heavy traffic."

Sam didn't wait for the what-do-we-do-now question. "No brainer, guys. I'm going to have to put a call into him and tell him my version of today's events right now. Give me five minutes to work out what I'm going to say." Sam had to do this. Her heart was in her mouth with just the thought of pressing his number on her phone. Either way, this call had to be made sooner rather than later. She continued, "Okay. I'm going to sound shook up, nervous and scared. Believe me, that won't be hard to do. I'll tell him about the Lexus and how I've been driving about since thinking everyone is following me. I'm super paranoid. He and I need to get our heads together and work out who the fuck it was. I'll tell him I won't do it tonight as I'm going to stay round at a friend's house and anyway, I've had a few drinks and can't drive even if he insists on meeting tonight. I will suggest the Crowne Plaza Hotel in Slough. It is a good plot for a team and always busy in the coffee lounge. Agreed?"

The boss and JW nodded in agreement. "Where are you going to call from? Do you want us to leave?" asked the boss.

"No, you can get me a drink from the bar please, just a prop you understand, and switch on the TV, I'll get my recording device set up." Five minutes later they were ready to rock and roll. Sam took a deep breath before saying, "Switch your phones off please and unplug the house phone." She made the introduction on the tape and pushed Coops' number on the phone.

"Hi, how's things with you?" he said.

"Not good, Coops, I'm scared. I was chased today from the

airport by someone, I don't know who, but it has scared the life out of me. I need to meet you, Coops, I need your help. I need to talk to someone I can trust. When are you coming back to the UK?"

"I'm at Marbella airport now waiting for my flight home. Look, calm down. Where are you right now?"

"I'm at a friend's house, she's a good friend, but she doesn't understand stuff, you know what I mean."

"I'm sure everything will be cool, but I can't make it tonight."

"What about tomorrow?" Sam said.

"Tomorrow is good. Where?"

"Do you know the Crowne Plaza in Slough near Heathrow?" she asked him.

"Yeah, I know it."

"Thanks, shall we say midday or earlier if you can make it?"

"Twelve is good for me."

"Thanks, you're a diamond, see you tomorrow, Coops. Night night." Sam switched off the device and gave a big sigh of relief.

"Bloody Oscar-winning performance, Sam," said the boss. "I don't know how you do it."

She smiled at him. "That wasn't play acting guv, it helps to be in the right frame of mind sometimes."

Sam's thoughts turned to her son, Bedbug, as she called James. She also started thinking about what-ifs. God, what if the Lexus had caught up with me? What if I'd crashed? What if I'd been assaulted? What if the real police had joined the chase? What if Coops had called me out as a cop on the phone? What if I was now lying in a hospital ICU? Better put a phone call into Rosie as she's on babysitting duty.

"Hello, how's things? James is fine, before you ask," Rosie

said.

"Yeah, good. Just finishing off my debrief and I'll be on the road. I've got an early start in the morning. Tell him I'll be home to tuck him in to bed."

"Of course," Rosie said. "I hope you're hungry."

"Starving, okay, got to go and get on the road. Bye," Sam said wondering what culinary delight awaited her.

Chapter 5: Of course, Mama

Arriving home, Sam called out to Rosie, "It's me. How is James?" Rosie was covering the one night Sam's mum was unable to cover childcare. Rosie greeted Sam in the hall, holding a welcome home glass of Cava. Upstairs, Sam heard global warfare coming from James' bedroom. The air was filled with the aroma of Rosie's cooking. Sniffing, she asked, "Italian?"

"Of course, mama, you can detect the smell of 'erbs in the air?" Rosie said in a fake Italian accent.

Imitating the accent Sam said, "No, I'm a detective and I can see the glass of Pinot on the worktop."

They both laughed and went into the kitchen. "Come on then, how was Spain?" Rosie asked as she turned the volume down on the quiz show she had been watching on TV.

"It had its moments, hun, but can we just have a chill out and a drink? I've had enough for today. I'm going up to see Bedbug." Rosie was one of the inner circle who knew something of what Sam was dealing with owing to the crash course in money laundering. Rosie instinctively knew it was not the time for Sam to share because of the need-to-know concept.

On entering James' bedroom, Sam said, "Hi darling, got a

kiss and a hug for your mum?"

He pressed the pause button on his PlayStation and the war instantly stopped. He rolled off his bed into Sam's open arms saying, "Don't worry, Mum. I haven't had any new paedophiles chatting me up." He wore a wide cheeky grin as he said it.

Sam was always telling James to be careful of strangers popping up online, pretending to be a kid looking for new mates. After her thirty seconds of love and hugs he was back on the battlefield with his friends fighting for survival, much the same as his mum's day. Out of the blue, the thought of her confrontation with Coops came to Sam as she was leaving the bedroom. Turning around, Sam looked him straight in his eyes, and said, "Be careful, James, some people aren't what they appear or say they are. Love you."

Closing the bedroom door, she joined Rosie in the kitchen. "Anything you can share or want to get off your chest?" Rosie said as if she had sensed something wasn't right.

"Not really, it's just this job. I met with Mister Big yesterday, and someone tried to follow me from the airport. It was no issue, an amateur job, even James could have lost him." Sam played it down without lying. After the delicious meal, Sam went to bed but didn't get much sleep.

Chapter 6: Sleepless

Sleepless nights are a part of this type of work. Last night Sam lay awake for hours thinking about her forthcoming meeting with Coops.

She was first at the briefing location, so waited in her car. JW showed up, followed shortly after by the boss. They walked into the reception area of the hotel while JW checked in. On seeing JW stepping into the lift, Sam received a text: room 536. On cue, she got up from her seat in reception and walked to the lift. As the lift doors were closing, Sam saw the boss standing outside but rather than reach for the 'open door' button, she let the lift doors close. He'll get the next one, she thought.

By the time all reached the room, JW had the kettle on and produced a fine coffee brand from his holdall, together with a creamer and demerara sugar. "Nice touch, JW, you'll make someone a lovely husband," Sam said.

There wasn't much to say at the briefing as everything had been said the previous evening and she had gone over the likely outcomes and scenarios. The what if this? What if that? Any old what if. Sam knew from previous experiences all plans would be out of the window after thirty seconds of sitting down. She just had to go with the flow and keep her poker face.

Briefing over, Sam got settled into a comfortable seat in a

corner of the reception. The two female surveillance operatives took up a position so they could video the currently empty seat opposite. The operatives looked like two ladies who met up for weekly coffee and sandwiches to catch up on the goss. One had several shopping bags and was producing items of clothing from the bags, trying to seek her friend's approval of her latest top.

Sam activated her recording device early and sat there flicking through the latest copy of a magazine she had picked up at the airport four days ago. *Has it only been four days? It feels like a lifetime.*

Sam saw Coops enter the reception area and scan round, presumably looking for her. She kept her head down, pretending not to notice him approach. *Keep your cards close to your chest, Sam.*

"Hello, Sam, fancy meeting you here," he said with a chuckle in his voice.

"You can chuckle, Mr Cooper, but I'm not in the mood for humour. I've not been that shook up for a long time. Someone was chasing me yesterday, and I don't know why or who it was. The only people who knew I was on that flight were Clifford, Hugo, Sergio and you. My head is in overdrive."

Sam was going to continue, but he interrupted. "Look, calm down, relax, take a deep breath. I asked him to follow you from the airport."

"You fucking what?" she snapped. "You had someone scare the shit out of me. You bastard. I'm out of here." Sam started to stand.

"Wait. I asked him to see where you went from the airport, not run you off the road. I like how you work and how you do business, but my man in the Lexus made an interesting comment. He said your drove like a professional, like a cop."

"That's the final straw, mister. I've spent almost six hundred thousand Euros with you. I've talked about turning your cash round, you can now forget all that. You have me followed and almost kill myself on the motorway. And now you're calling me a cop. Fuck off."

The ante on the table was now at its highest. Her heart was racing, and her pulse was off the scale.

"So where did you learn to drive, Sam?"

Sam held his gaze for a few seconds before she said, "I told you the other night, Mister Cooper, there is lots you don't know about me, yet. So, pin your ears back. When I lived out in Cape Town my then partner, who was a member of the South African Special Forces Brigade or Recces as they are known over there, taught me how to drive in the event of someone trying to carjack me, and for your information and that of your dog from yesterday, he also taught me how to use a gun if I need to. I can drive better than anyone out there and that includes that thug you set on me yesterday. So go and tell your thug that he had his pants pulled down by a blonde who has more talent in her little finger than he has in his whole body. Now if you're done, I'm going. I'd like to say it's been nice knowing you but that would be a lie."

Coops had just experienced a Sam flash bang. Sam started to gather her jacket, bag and magazine. "If you wanted to find anything out about me, all you had to do was ask. I don't know how the cops work or where they get their money from, but I doubt they would give you almost six hundred thousand Euros of their cash. If you'll excuse me, Mister Cooper, goodbye." She set off to walk out on him.

"Just hang on, I owe you an apology, Sam. I just wanted to be sure of you, that's all it was. You're a tough cookie and I realise I've gone about this the wrong way. Can we start again?"

Sam stopped and played one more card. "Why would I wipe the slate clean? What's in it for me? We can't work together if there is no trust. I don't know. Let me have some time to think things over, I'll give you a call." With that, she walked out on him, jumped into her Beemer and hit the road again, ensuring nothing was following.

Chapter 7: Hoffman

S am was way more relaxed when she attended the debrief than she was at the earlier briefing. What a difference two hours can make. The boss and JW were enthusiastically over the moon with her handling of the meeting and couldn't wait to hear what was said on the phone tap. Sam was thinking of the next phase. She needed an office environment where she could meet Coops. It had to look real, for Sam knew the picture needed a few more brush strokes to convince Coops all was tickety- boo.

She also knew someone, somewhere, would have suitable covert premises that could be used and burned on this multi-agency operation. JW got on the phone to his network around the country. True to form, he found one just outside the M25 in Kent. JW took care of all the logistics and setting up the 'office.' He contacted their undercover cousins in Germany and secured the services of a German undercover officer with a legend in finance, who went under the name of Hoffman.

In due course, JW reported that as expected, Coops had got on the phone immediately after his meeting with Sam. His first call was to Terrance Walker. He brought him up to speed and passed on Sam's message about his lack of talent. Walker warned Coops to tread carefully.

On Sam's part, she gave it four or five days before texting Coops, letting him know that she would like to have a meeting with him at her office if he was still interested. Owing to the phone tap, they knew he was out in the Canaries on business. Sam could put the meeting off for a further four or five days by which time the office would be up and running with props and staff, including Clifford the accountant and Hoffman the financial wizard. Coops texted back after an hour or so explaining he'd be back in the country in six days. Perfect, Sam thought. She texted him again, telling him to call when back to arrange a meeting. Not only did this give the team time to set the scene, it gave her some time with Bedbug.

The following week was a well-earned period of recuperation. Sam returned Coops' text confirming a meeting on Friday at the Kent office, giving him the address and post code. The stage was set.

"Sam, great to see you again, how have you been keeping?"

"I'm good thanks, Coops, let me introduce you to Clifford, my accountant. The others are my trusted office staff. The guy in the side office is Hoffman, my German genius. It's rumoured he could make the Eiffel Tower disappear and no one would notice."

Between Sam, Clifford and Hoffman they bamboozled Coops into believing they had a foolproof system of laundering his dirty money via several bank accounts within the European Union including Cyprus, and from there into a clean account in the Cayman Islands. To show good faith and as a free test, Sam suggested they did a small amount of fifty thousand pounds sterling. She told him she would underwrite the money if anything went wrong. This was one game of poker she knew she would win because she was cheating again. His money would be secured in an account controlled by the City of London Serious Fraud Department in a friendly bank in the Cayman Islands.

Sam spent five full days giving evidence from the witness box in the Old Bailey's number one court. She read statements, pocket notebooks and transcripts. In cross-examination by the defence barristers, she repeatedly pointed out all her recorded conversations with Coops avoided the use of direct questions and were entirely legal. The operation ran for eighteen months. Six million pounds in cash and every piece of property he had in Europe and in the UK were seized under the Proceeds of Crime Act. The details of how they achieved that are secret. They may have to be used again in a future operation.

Coops and the Spaniard were handed lengthy sentences to be spent in a six by ten prison cell. He should have called Sam's bluff when she went to walk out of their heated meeting in the Crowne Plaza Hotel in Slough or better still, he should have listened and taken the advice of his mate, the private eye. The guy who was too slow to catch Sam.

Chapter 8: Bristol Fraudster

Life Before Samantha

Dom attended many courses during his undercover career, including a 'Firearms Familiarisation Course' with the nation's elite Armed Forces and Special Forces. He loved getting back amongst those lads and the piss taking and banter that formed the character of some of the greatest men he had the pleasure to know. However, there were some firearms around that he hadn't picked up or used. They included flash bang grenades. On a course with Special Forces, he got the opportunity to use one. Having thrown many conventional hand grenades, he pulled the pin and lobbed it in the prescribed military method, like a cricket delivery into the target area. A conventional grenade has a fuse which burns for several seconds and then you get the big bang. Flash bangs don't have a slow burning fuse. They virtually explode instantly, thereby creating flash, noise, smoke, and disorientation. Dom's grenade exploded in mid-air, sending fragments of the grenade casing in all directions. One fragment found its way down the collar of the instructor's smock, causing superficial burns to his neck and shoulder. He was very forgiving, thank God – after pointing out that he had been in combat and under fire in various parts of the world and not been scratched. This event happened many years ago, but Dom still opened parcels sent to his address with caution. Just in case.

What has this to do with the Bristol Fraudster?

Detective Inspector Kath Murdock called Dom whilst he was on this firearms course with Special Forces. As she headed up his department, he took the call. She told him another force had requested him for a role that suited one of his personas. They wanted an undercover officer who could play the role of a corrupt Detective Sergeant. Dom had the ability to dress up and carry himself off as a businessman, or dress down as a lorry driver, and all stations in between. Dom was in two minds. He had to decide between three more days with what he regarded as his military family owing to his former military life or go back and do his day job which he loved. Rather than sit on it and think things over, he told the boss he'd drive back that night and do the job.

The days on the course always finished with cleaning the weapons they had fired during the day; a task Dom did not enjoy. He would often be asked with his background in firearms and as a weapons instructor why he'd not applied to join the firearms department. His stock answer was, "Because I hate cleaning them." After dinner Dom said farewell to his fellow colleagues on the course and the instructors, who all understood the need for him to react to a phone call and disappear.

On the drive home, Dom started to think about the role he was about to undertake. Playing the role of a corrupt cop wouldn't be that difficult. He'd seen and unfortunately worked alongside wonky cops, some of whom had featured in television programmes such as 'Panorama' and ended up serving long jail time. So, finding a role model would not be a difficult task. There was a lot of media coverage at the time about police corruption, canteen culture and investigative journalists infiltrating police environments to grab the headlines. He was confident he could paint a picture of a dirty cop. His mind turned to a name for this corrupt cop. Playing the game in his head, he came up with Ben. This was the name of a character in a television programme who was a dodgy police officer.

The next morning Dom and his boss, Kath, met up at the off-site. An off-site is a covert office not located on police premises. It is used by cover officers as their office and UCOs use it for any administrative tasks. Some are offices in a building containing other businesses or a unit on an industrial estate. They always have a covert front. Real police never visit nor are made aware of the location.

After a quick cuppa and chat about another operation, they jumped into their separate vehicles and set off on the road to their friends in a neighbouring force. Dom was busy taking and making phone calls for most of the journey. Just before ten thirty, he turned the phone to silent. Now, he could see who was calling and choose whether to take the call or let it go to answer phone. He could now challenge himself on Radio Two's 'Pop Master' without interruption. Dom fancied himself as a pop aficionado and would often irritate his fellow passengers by shouting out the song title, singer, or band in the first few notes.

'Pop Master' over, Dom relished his second place today with twenty-four points as he pulled into a parking space at the off-site. Dom got out of his car as Kath pulled in. He decided to leave his phone on silent for the imminent meeting with Daz and a DI from his Financial Investigation Department. Dom knew Darren, or Daz as he liked to be known, from past deployments. Waiting for Kath to join him, Dom let her finish her phone call. He saw she had her phone to her ear as she got out of her car and walked towards him. Kath finished her call with, "Love you too. Bye."

Smiling, Dom enquired, "New fella in your life, Kath?"

"Behave yourself, big ears, it was my mum. I'm having some time off men for now."

Kath was in her early thirties and had recently come out of a long-term relationship with another cop that wasn't going anywhere. He was divorced, with a couple of teenage kids who didn't get on with Kath and made life uncomfortable for her at every opportunity. Her ex found himself between a rock and a hard place when trying to keep both sides of the equation happy. This would often end up with Kath taking herself off to the local motel for a night or two until tempers had settled down. Eventually she rented a flat and two nights became a week and the next time after a row a bit longer until the relationship died, or as Kath would say, killed by his kids. Kath was attractive and wouldn't be on the available list for long.

Daz waved to them as they approached his office and greeted them at the door. He introduced them to Paul Timms, who was a Detective Inspector on the Financial Investigations Department. The kettle was already on with an assortment of tea and coffee available. The traditional collection of coffee and tea-stained mugs and cups were on a tray next to the boiling kettle.

"I'll let you help yourselves to tea or coffee, Kath, as apparently and according to Dom, I can't make tea because I was born south of Watford Gap Services," Daz said as he and Paul took up a couple of chairs at a round table in the corner of the office. Paul sat facing a neat and tidy stack of papers. After fixing a couple of teas, Kath and Dom took their seats and Paul began with the story. He slid colour photocopies of a head shot of a male across the table. The man in the photo looked to be in his late thirties, with a Mediterranean appearance: black hair, slim face, and dark eyes, a good-looking guy. As he distributed the photocopies, he introduced the mystery man.

"This handsome gentleman is Alessandro Rossi. He answers to the name of Aless, not Alex, that really pisses him off. His parents are from Sicily, moved to the UK thirty odd, maybe forty years ago. After a few years Aless was born. He speaks English, Italian, French and German. He has a very nice lifestyle and lives in a penthouse apartment in a new development just off the city centre."

Paul paused for a moment as he fumbled through his file of papers. Dom took the opportunity for a quick one liner. "Swipe left or right, Kath?"

Kath lightly laughed. "Piss off, Dom, you prick."

Paul continued as he looked across at Dom and Kath with a confused expression as he tried to work out the in joke between the two officers. "Aless is a fraudster, a very good fraudster, but he got himself mixed up with two Eastern European like-minded fraudsters who skipped the country when it was all coming on top and left Aless to face the music. We're in the throes of issuing international arrest warrants for the Europeans but we don't hold out much hope of finding them."

Dom's expression changed from listening inquisitively to one of uncertainty and surprise. Before he could voice his concern, Paul went on, "Don't panic, Dom." Paul added, "We're not sending you out to the fleshpots of deepest darkest Europe or want you to learn the inside outs of complex fraud. We need you, as I explained to Kath, to be a bent copper. Detective Constable Mark Turner, who is the case officer, was processing Aless prior to being released on bail when Turner was offered a bribe by Aless to crash and wreck the case. Mark is a switched-on lad and made a note in his pocketbook and came to see me prior to releasing Aless on bail. I had a quick chat with Daz. He and I came up with a bit of a game plan and here you are, Dom. What we want is for you to develop a dialogue and a relationship via Mark with Aless and tell us what he wants. Mark's on standby to put a call into Aless and introduce you as his Detective Sergeant who has access to all the exhibits, court files and ongoing enquiries and you might be able to help."

Dom was nodding as Paul finished, then said, "Okay, sounds straightforward at this stage. Off the top of my head, I'll need a warrant card and a CID job car. I'm thinking of using the name Benjamin, Ben for short, and a surname of Smith. I don't imagine for a moment I'll have to disclose or expose any other documentation, so a thin layer of covertness should be sufficient at this early stage. Let's arrange contact and see where we go from there."

Kath piped in with the important stuff. "Are all the authorities in place, Daz? I just need to satisfy myself we're good to go on that side."

"Yeah, just being finished off now, we have agreement on what we have discussed here. Once signed sealed and delivered, I'll get Mark to call Aless and introduce Ben who can call him later today, if that works for you two."

Dom and Kath both agreed to Daz's timeline and plan. Dom

added, "I'd like to have a quick chat with Mark before he makes the call."

Daz said, "I knew you would, mate. He's in the canteen down the road, ready and waiting for you. You can nip across there when you're ready. I've asked him to take you up to the photographer and get a photo for the warrant card."

Chapter 9: People Watching

D om left the others in the office and made his way to the canteen to introduce himself to Mark and discuss what he was going to say to Aless. Dom had turned up for the briefing wearing a polo shirt and ideally, he should be wearing a collar and tie for his warrant card picture. So, Mark's first job working with an undercover officer was to exchange his collar and tie for Dom's polo shirt. Both men had a chuckle when changing in the gents' loo. Mark was smaller than Dom and the polo shirt hung off him, whereas Dom looked like the Incredible Hulk in the borrowed shirt. Both were happy to get their own clothes back after the photoshoot.

After a short time, Mark was told to make the call and get the ball rolling. Dom sat by Mark as he made the recorded phone call. Once the call was ended and the tape switched off, Dom shook hands with Mark and congratulated him on a good job. Dom returned to the off-site to report to Daz and confirm when his warrant card would be ready for collection. Daz was going to collect the card from HQ in the next hour or so. Dom wanted to make first contact with Aless from a phone box on Mark's home force ground. In that way, Aless would see the local dial code come up on his mobile. Kath took a copy of the back page from the signed authority for her records and set off back to her office.

Dom suggested he would kill some time in the city centre. He was a great people watcher. When he went shopping with his wife, Judy, he would always wait outside the shops 'people watching'. He didn't only study the passing members of the public and in seconds guess at their status and standing on the planet, he would nick little bits of their behaviour without their consent or knowledge and weave it into his different personas. Dom knew he could be distracted from his game by an attractive female passing by. But it was always a distraction, nothing more. Dom didn't have the time nor inclination to stray outside of his marriage. Besides, he knew Judy accepted his lifestyle with its frequent absences from home and often called into action at the drop of a hat. Not many wives would.

Within an hour, Daz called Dom informing him that the warrant card was ready for collection. The call disturbed Dom's thoughts on the passing case studies and reflections on his home life and how he was going to play his role. He didn't want to tell Aless how to wreck the case against him, Aless needed him to clearly set out what he wanted, and not what Dom wanted. Once Aless had made his demands and mentioned what he wanted, Dom could open the dialogue without falling into the trap of conducting an interview or acting as an agent provocateur. He decided that he would open their first conversation with a simple short sentence, 'How can I help you, Aless?'

Dom went back to Daz's office and stayed just long enough to pick up his new warrant card. The photo looked good, no indication of the stress on the shirt buttons. He picked up a recording device and sufficient tapes to cover several phone calls if required and any meetings that might be arranged on the hurry-up. Just before bidding Daz goodbye, Dom reminded him that he would need a CID job car when he drove to meetings with Aless.

Just before Dom crossed the county border, he pulled into a residential street and found a phone box outside a parade of shops that conveniently had a layby outside. Before getting out of his car, he placed a tape into the recorder and made the standard introduction and switched the device off. Inside the phone box he inhaled the familiar stench of cigarettes and urine and wondered how many drug deals had been arranged from the box. He switched the device on and rang Aless on the number he had been given by Mark. The phone rang four or five times before it was picked up. The voice on the other end introduced himself. "Hello, Alessandro."

"Hi, Alessandro, My name's Ben. I'm a friend of Mark's. How can I help you?"

"Hello, Ben, thanks for calling. Call me Aless. Has Mark explained my situation?"

"He's told me that you've been nicked on a fraud job and you wanted a hand. That's about it." Dom waited for Aless to fill the silence.

"Okay, Ben, I need to meet you. I'm not comfortable talking over the phone with someone I don't know or even met. This might be a set up. So, let's have a sit down and feel each other out."

Without hesitation, Dom said, "My thoughts exactly, Alessandro. You could be working for a national newspaper, trying to get reporter of the year with the scalp of a copper. You could be an undercover cop looking to trap a hard-working officer with a bit of a reputation who's had a few complaints against him for this and that. Don't forget, my friend, I know

45

how these things work. So yeah, let's have a meeting and take it from there. If you think it smells or I do, we walk away from each other, no harm done. No one else at the meeting, just you and me. Agreed?"

Alessandro agreed with everything Dom said to him and arranged to meet up in the next few days when Ben could arrange to slide away for an hour or so. He told Aless that he was giving evidence in court the day after tomorrow and he would meet him that afternoon and would call him that morning to confirm the venue. Dom hung up the phone, switched off the device and slipped it into his pocket. He was glad to get out of the box and breathe fresh air. He didn't hang around people watching. He had already worked out the local talent. As he set off on his journey home, he called Daz and debriefed him about the phone call with Aless and suggested Leigh Delamere Services on the M4 motorway. Service stations are easy plots to cover with a surveillance team for vehicle movement and control of the subject once they are out of their car on foot. Daz agreed. He would debrief Paul and they would sign everything up prior to the deployment on Friday.

Chapter 10: Yeah, Einstein

Friday morning arrived and Dom drove across the force border to make his call to Aless from a phone box. Not recovered fully from his previously selected phone box, he headed for the city centre. The new tape was placed into the recorder followed by the usual introduction, and into the box. He brought up Aless's number and pressed the call button.

"Hello, Alessandro speaking."

"Hi, Aless, It's Ben. Can you make Leigh Delamere Services on the M4 for two o'clock today?"

"Bloody hell, Ben, that's a bit of a drag for me, can you come further along the M4?"

"Not really, mate, I'm at work and have to be able to respond if I get a shout. I've been cancelled from court, so I'm stuck. We can leave it until next week if you want?"

There were a few moments of silence. "I don't want to hang about till next week, Ben. I want to get this done and dusted. Okay, what side of the motorway?"

Dom smiled at the promising verbals from Aless, then said, "Do it on the westbound?"

"Yeah, westbound, that's in the direction of Wales, yeah?" Aless asked.

Dom smiled again. "Yeah, Einstein, towards Welsh Wales.

I'll see you just inside the entrance at two."

"How will I know you or recognise you, Ben?"

"You won't, but I know you to look at. I've had a look at your custody photograph. Just be there for two, I'll find you. Okay?"

"Oh yeah, I didn't think of that. Not the best picture. Yeah, Two o'clock, Ben. Look forward to seeing you."

The phone went dead, and Dom switched off the device. Back in his car he made a quick call to Daz to update him and to give the operational team as much time as possible to plan the deployment. Daz called Dom back after about half an hour, telling him that he had booked a meeting room as a briefing location in the Travel Lodge Hotel on the eastbound carriageway, and he would be there with the DI by twelve to debrief and brief. He would have a job car there for him. As the call came to an end Dom asked, "Eastbound, Daz, is that towards London?"

"Yeah, towards London. What's that all about?"

"Nothing, just my little joke. I'll explain when I see you, mate."

Later that day Dom was sitting in his car observing the entrance to the Travel Lodge Hotel. He saw Daz and Paul walking across the car park and into the hotel. After a few minutes Dom's phone buzzed, indicating he had received a text message. Picking the phone up from the front passenger seat, he read the message:

Your car needs a wash lol. Meeting room in the name of Anglo Products ask at reception for directions.

That was Dom's signal to join them. He collected his holdall from the back seat and walked into the hotel. Glancing at a maroon Ford Escort car parked to the left of the doorway, Dom had two thoughts. One, that this car had been neglected by its current owner and needed some TLC. Secondly, this was his job car.

The middle-aged smartly dressed lady in corporate uniform was behind the reception desk tapping away on her keyboard. Dom said, "Excuse me, I've got a meeting with Anglo Products here today, can you direct me please?"

Looking up, she said, "Hello, where did you come from? I didn't see you come in."

She had a pleasing and welcoming smile. Returning to her computer, she tapped the keyboard then pointed towards a door to her right. With that, she sat upright, pulling her shoulders back and revealing her figure as she continued, "Yes, they are in meeting room one. I'll buzz the door for you and it's the first door on the right."

Dom looked in the direction she had indicated then turned towards the door and thanked her. He got the impression that had he got into a conversation with this lady it would one be full of innuendo, and she would hold him there forever. So he made his way to the internal door without any delay and waited for the automated click as the lock was released.

Daz and Paul were sitting and were all set up around the small conference table in the centre of the room. There was the usual collection of cups and the ingredients for tea or coffee on a small round table in the corner. Paul produced a packet of chocolate chip cookies from his briefcase. Paul was famous for his cookie biscuits. Dom, in business like fashion, produced his pocket notebook, PNB, and two mini cassette tapes from his rucksack. He then arranged hot drinks for Paul, Daz and himself. Settling down at the conference table, he helped himself to a couple of cookies, with Paul's blessing, and read out his notes. He placed the tapes into separate exhibit bags supplied by Daz which he then signed and sealed before handing them to Paul. Dom completed the entry in his PNB that he'd handed over the tape exhibits and invited Paul to sign his PNB.

The briefing for the meeting with Aless was short, sharp and to the point. The main aim was to get Aless to spit out what he wanted. Paul told Dom he could ask for twenty-thousand pounds. They agreed that he would want ten-thousand upfront at the next meeting as a sign of good will and commitment. Daz handed Dom a different, more techie recording device for the meeting, then instructed him on its use. It was a simple on or off device. Even Dom could manage this. It was a long way from the days of a reel-to-reel tape deck taped in the small of his back. Technical advancement in the type of devices used by undercover officers had gone in leaps and bounds over the years. Undoubtedly, they will continue to become more sophisticated. He also handed Dom a new burner phone. Daz had charged up the phone and stuck thirty pounds of credit on it. Dom went into the settings and selected the classic bell ringtone. He then made a note of his new phone number on the corner of a sheet of A4 paper and ripped it from the sheet. He placed the bit of paper into the back pocket of his trousers.

Paul moved on to the surveillance team and confirmed they would be there just to record evidence the meeting took place. This was a normal 'best evidence' practice when a team were building an evidence case against a suspect. Paul also handed Dom a key to a Ford car. The key and fob had a yellow plastic tag attached which at some point would have had the vehicle make, model and registration on it. Now it simply said 'Escort' written in black permanent marker pen. Paul started to tell him where the car was parked. Dom cut him short and picked up the key. "Yep, cheers boss. I think I spied it on the way in here." Dom left the meeting room and out via reception. The receptionist attempted to engage him in conversation, but Dom wasn't having it. He apologised and said he was in a hurry and disappeared into the car park.

Chapter 11: Leigh Delamere

L eigh Delamere service station is located between junctions seventeen and eighteen on the M4. Dom set off in his shabby looking Escort east on the M4 from the service station in the direction of London. At junction seventeen he first slipped off and then back on in the other direction, giving himself plenty of time to take up his position in the entrance at ten to two. Before getting out of his car he reactivated the recording device and stated the time, date, and his location. Walking across to the entrance, he stood just inside the door so he could monitor every person who came in. At ten past two Aless hadn't turned up. Dom was confident he hadn't missed him. He used a phone box outside the entrance to the building and punched in Aless's number. Dom heard one ring tone before the phone was answered. "Where the fuck are you?" Dom asked, sounding pissed off.

"I'm in the car park watching the doorway to make sure you've not brought the police with you."

"You've got two minutes to get here before I rev up and fuck off. I'm stood by the plastic pot plants just inside the door. Two minutes." Dom hung up and checked the time.

The surveillance team would be updating the boss and Daz, so there was no need for him to worry about that. Within two minutes he saw Aless walk through the entrance doors. Dom was the only person standing by the faux flower arrangement and Aless walked directly towards him. Aless nodded in Dom's direction. Dom returned the greeting without either man speaking. Aless then nodded towards the gents' toilet. Dom guessed it was a signal to follow so that was what he did. Once inside, Aless gestured for Dom to open his coat and he quickly patted Dom down. Satisfied Dom wasn't wired, he again nodded towards the exit. Dom followed again as he led him into the restaurant area. They joined the queue at the drinks counter. Still not a word passed between them. Aless pointed at the tea and coffee with the index finger of his right hand. I'll play your stupid game, Dom thought and pointed at the coffee. They grabbed a couple of coffees that Aless paid for and walked over to a table of Aless's choice in the far corner. Aless positioned himself at the table giving a full view of the restaurant seating area. Dom sat with his back to the room, a position he would not pick in normal circumstances, but he had a full surveillance team covering his back. They sat and Aless stared at Dom for ten or fifteen seconds without a word. Dom decided he'd open the conversation. "How is it I can help you, Aless?"

Aless continued to stare at Dom as if he was in a trance. Dom waited for him to speak. He didn't.

"Are you okay, Aless?"

Aless rocked his head gently from side to side. Dom took that as a negative. Dom wondered, Where's the on and off switch on this guy. I need to move this along.

"This thing will only work if you talk, Aless, we can't do this on shakes and nods of the head. We need words. If you're going to carry on like this, I'm off, mate. It's up to you."

Aless broke his silence. "This might be a trap, you could be recording me, the table might be bugged."

"You just searched me in the bogs. You picked the table, and I could have the same reservations about this meeting you have. Let me tell you this. If this is a setup and you're here to take me down, you'll go down before me. I'll guarantee it."

Aless stood up. "Okay, let's go for a walk around the car park. I'll feel more comfortable out there."

Chapter 12: Looks Like a Cop Car

Dom gulped a mouth full of coffee and stood up. Both men walked out and began their promenade up and down the parked cars. At one point, Aless stopped and pulled Dom by the elbow. He nodded in the direction of a maroon Ford Escort. "Fuck, that looks like a cop car!"

Dom took the key from his pocket and pressed the fob which activated the door locks and a flash of the indicators on the Escort.

Grinning, Dom said, "Yep, so it is. How do you think I got here?" He hoped that would lighten the mood.

Aless was still careful and cagy about what he said and didn't say. He talked around the subject without mentioning anything specific. Dom didn't feel Aless said enough to get the job home at court. But didn't want to drive the job forward. Dom told Aless that they had to trust each other and stop the double talk and suspecting they might be setting each other up. Aless agreed and suggested they meet in a sauna. Dom had heard stories of villains meeting in swimming pools to ensure they couldn't be recorded. This was Dom's first encounter with a similar request. Thinking quickly and knowing there wasn't complete trust between them, Dom used it to his advantage. He pointed out to Aless how it would look if he was pictured coming out of a sauna with a crook. "It might look great on the front page of a daily newspaper but not on my personal file."

Aless continued to reassure Dom that it wasn't a setup, and he was serious about wrecking the case against him. Dom realised he had Aless on the hook. Aless was now trying to convince Dom that it was not a setup. Dom needed to keep this advantage. Like a chess master, Dom was thinking two or three moves ahead if he agreed to Aless's suggestion of the sauna. After some rapid thinking, Dom agreed. Aless informed him he would arrange a venue for their next meeting. This didn't sit comfortably with Dom as he would be giving up control, but the boss and Daz might decide that the thought of having a sauna was a bad idea. So, it would be a non-starter. He didn't want Aless to slip backwards in the trust stakes, so he went along with it, for now. Dom decided that this was the right time to sort the money out. Aless stopped by his red Porsche.

"Right, let's get down to my fee. I don't know too much right now but what I do know is what your liberty is worth to you. I don't think you'll enjoy jail time or the food. So, these are my terms. I want ten grand at our next meeting and ten grand when I give you what you want."

Aless, without skipping a heartbeat, agreed.

They shook hands and Dom slipped Aless the piece of paper on which he had written down a mobile number. He emphasised to Aless that this was the only number to contact him. He was not to share the number with anyone or use the phone for any other business. Once more, Aless agreed. Aless drove out of the services in his Porsche at the head of a convoy of nondescript surveillance vehicles. Dom knew the surveillance team would stay with Aless to see where he went and what he did after their meeting. If it proved to be of non-evidential value, the team would stand down.

Retracing his earlier drive but in the opposite direction, Dom now made his way west on the motorway for a junction where he exited, drove around the roundabout for a full circle then headed east, arriving back at the Travel Lodge. To Dom's relief there was a male manning the reception. Dom noticed his name badge was 'Derek,' who was less chatty than the middle-aged lady. Dom was back with Paul and Daz within seconds. Everyone sat down and Dom gave a verbal debrief. Before doing so, he looked for the cookies. His hopes were dashed as he saw the empty packet sticking out of the small bin by the tea making table. Paul was happy how things had gone, even though Aless had not made it clear what he wanted, but he wanted something and was happy to pay twenty grand for it. There was a light-hearted conversation about the next meeting being held in a sauna and the difficulties of capturing the verbals on a device.

Paul said, "What were you thinking, Dom? Agreeing to a meeting in a sauna!"

Dom thought for a moment and said, "I thought with the modern advancements in recording equipment they might be able to do something. You know, find us a bit of spy kit. What about sticking the thing in a flip flop?"

That suggestion was laughed out of the room by Paul and Daz, after which Dom kept his thoughts to himself and left it to the techies. Before parting company, Dom did his administration, and the paperwork was completed and signed. Paul wanted to talk over the next meeting between Dom and Aless with his boss and work out a policy and strategy that would be written up in his policy book and put in front of the Authorising Officer, AO, if necessary. He assured them would have a decision by end of play today and Daz would relay that decision to Dom.

Dom set off home looking forward to the weekend. He had a few things bubbling but hopefully would have a bit of family time even though things weren't too good at home. Nothing too serious but he did wonder if he took Judy for granted. Then his thoughts turned to the kids who he adored and if anything would wreck the marriage, it would be Dom's job, not Dom, the father per se.

His son was playing football for the local team and that became the focus of his weekend. Dom had made a promise to himself, as he had done on previous weeks, not to get too loud on the touch line. A promise he broke every time. Judy had a list of DIY jobs that he would do his best to avoid and began thinking of excuses she had not heard before of why he couldn't do them. The journey home was torturous. Friday evening was not a time to drive across the county. It took him an hour longer than it should have. But Judy had prepared a chilli con carne with a cheap and cheerful bottle of Rioja. Dom was no connoisseur of wine. If it contained alcohol, it was good with him.

Halfway down the Rioja, Daz called Dom. Everything was good to go with the sauna meeting. It had been authorised this sauna meeting would be uncorroborated, no contemporaneous recording, and Dom would attempt to retrospectively corrobo-rate at subsequent meetings when it would be possible to use a recording device. Nothing out of the ordinary with this tactic and Dom was relaxed about it.

Dom spent Saturday fixing the backdoor lock. It was at best a twenty-minute job, but using all his skill, knowledge, and undercover training, he dragged it out all afternoon. Judy was delighted that she could turn the key in one smooth movement rather than wiggling the key in the lock for ages before she could open the door. Sunday morning, and his lad's football had arrived. Dom was more excited about the game than his lad. As they were getting into the family car, Judy reminded Dom about his behaviour on the touchline. Dom gave her that 'who me?' look.

Knowing he was expecting a call from Aless, Dom slipped the mobile used to contact him into his jacket. Dom didn't like missing calls or ignoring calls from the subjects of an operation. He thought the optics didn't look right if his phone went to answer phone nine times out of ten, especially at weekends.

The game kicked off on time. It took two minutes for Dom to break his promises to stay quiet, so he ended up standing on his own. Just before the halftime whistle, Aless's phone rang in Dom's pocket. It wasn't very covert to start producing recording equipment on a recreational ground, but he wanted to respond to Aless's call. Dom answered the call.

Chapter 13: I'm at the Football

"Hi, Aless, everything okay?" Dom asked.

"Yeah, good thanks, Ben. I've got a venue for our meeting."

Dom interrupted, "Mate, can I stop you there? I'm at the football with my lad. Can I call you a bit later when I get away?" As if on cue the halftime whistle sounded, and a ripple of applause rang out. Dom shouted, "Good half, lads."

Aless must have heard as he said, "Yeah, no worries, Ben, call me later. What's the score?"

"Two up, I'll call you later, mate. Thanks."

Dom slid the phone back into his jacket pocket and walked across to where the team had congregated. Dom stood on the periphery of the gathering as their manager gave his words of wisdom and encouragement. Even those who hadn't played well got a pat on the back. Dom wasn't a fan of that but understood.

On returning home, Dom took himself off to the dining room with his phone and recording device. This was sanctioned by Judy because she had come to understand and tolerate the idiosyncrasies of Dom and his damn job. His son and daughter were of an age now that they knew if Dad went in there and shut the door it was work stuff. Dom set up the device and made the usual introduction, adding that he received a call from Aless and was not able to record the conversation, but he would refer to the call to back corroborate their earlier conversation.

"Hi, Aless, sorry about earlier when you called, mate, I was with my lad at the football. We won four-one. My lad got two. A chip of the old block."

"When we were walking round the car park the other day, I had a feeling you used to play football by the way you walked. Am I right?"

Dom thought, Where has that come from? I need to stay in my legend, and part of that legend is I'm divorced, the way things are going, it could be true. "Yeah, I played a bit in my day, mate. I was never going to make it big time, but he's got a chance if the right coach gets hold of him. But he lives with his mum, and she's not got the foresight to encourage him. I only get to see him at weekends and the odd weekday here and there. Anyway, enough about footy, what's happening with you and me?"

Aless told Dom he wanted to meet up tomorrow at Hengrove Park Leisure Centre in Bristol around mid-afternoon, where they could discuss the details of his case. He said he would meet Dom in the car park and take him into the Leisure Centre. Dom agreed, and once he'd finished his call with Aless he called Daz and briefed him. Dom arranged to call into the off-site at ten o'clock on his way to the Leisure Centre to do the necessary with him and Paul.

At five minutes to ten the next day, Dom knocked on the door of Daz's secure and clandestine office. Both Daz and Paul greeted him. They looked like they had been double busy over the last few hours organising a surveillance team and Dom's briefing. Dom helped himself to an exhibit bag for the tape.

Once signed and sealed, he placed it on the table ready for Paul. Daz went into a smaller office just off the main office to make a phone call. Dom put the kettle on and hoped that Paul was running to form with the chocolate chip cookies. Dom's hopes were answered as he heard Paul say, "Choccy chips in my bag, Dom, if you fancy one with your tea."

"Cheers, boss," Dom said reaching into the bag and grabbing a new sealed packet.

Dom suggested that after the sauna meeting, he was going to suggest they, Dom and Aless, sit and have a coffee in the lounge area. He would tell Aless to buy a new burner phone for himself and just have a conversation and get him to relax. Hopefully, he would get him to repeat his demands. Just as they had finished their briefing, Dom's burner phone rang. Dom moved into the small office at whilst pulling his recording equipment from his bag and activating it. Aless confirmed the meeting for one o'clock and said he would meet Dom in the car park. Dom set off at around eleven o'clock, giving himself plenty of time to reach the venue.

Chapter 14: The Leisure Centre

At five to one Dom returned to the Leisure Centre and followed the arrows to navigate the rows of parked cars. He spotted Aless's red Porsche and pulled into a vacant space close by. Before getting out of his vehicle, Dom activated the recording device. Both men grabbed their sports bags and locked their cars before greeting each other by shaking hands. Aless approached the reception desk and picked up two complimentary towels. He paid for both and led the way towards the male locker room. Dom got the impression that this was not Aless's first visit to the Centre. The locker room was large and spacious, divided by dark mahogany lockers and benches that created smaller areas. There were a few TVs fixed to the walls around the room. Aless stopped and put his bag down in one of the areas and invited Dom to do likewise. Both men selected a locker and began to change into their swim shorts. As Aless was changing, he engaged Dom in small talk but seemed to watch Dom. Dom knew he was looking for some sort of recording device. Before Dom put on his swim shorts, he tossed them towards Aless. "Do you want to check these?"

Aless laughed and caught the shorts in mid-air, squeezing them between both hands, then tossed them back at Dom. Aless reciprocated by inviting Dom to check his swim shorts. There were now two naked men acting like schoolboys, throwing their shorts around. Dom thought the bizarre thought, No one told me I would have to do this one day as an undercover cop. Securing their lockers and picking up their towels, Aless took the lead into the wet area.

Entering the sauna, they found they were not alone. Sitting in a corner was an extremely overweight man who didn't move a muscle or say a word as the two men sat on the bench opposite him. Dom and Aless said nothing and in Dom's case, he hoped the guy would get uncomfortable with the silence and piss off. After a silent five minutes, Aless decided that the mass opposite wasn't going to move so he nodded towards the door and stood up. Once outside the sauna, he jokingly said to Dom, "Do you think he's alive? Come on, let's get in the pool."

Both men lowered themselves into the shallow end of the swimming pool and walked until the water was up to their necks. They stopped by the side of the pool. The only other person in the pool was an elderly lady doing slow lengths on the other side. Aless took a deep breath as if he was about to dive under the water. He exhaled and the floodgates opened. "I need you to get my laptop, passport, twenty-five thousand in cash and a blue file which were all seized by the police together with other bits of crap when I was arrested, and when they searched my gaff. They have three of my laptops, but two of them have nothing incriminating on them. I want the HP, the one with all the juicy stuff on it. Can you do that?"

Nodding but stifling his amazement at Aless's sudden outburst, Dom said, "Everything is doable, Aless, for the right price. Now you've told me what you want, let me ask you something. Have you got the money I asked for?"

"It's locked in the car, Ben."

Dom now had Aless's words, but not on tape. He knew he needed more to get this job home at court. He knew he needed corroborated evidence. As a leading barrister once said, 'If it isn't written, officer, it wasn't said.' Unfortunately, historically some police officers have fabricated evidence under the heading of 'noble corruption' to 'fit criminals up.' Dom always had a problem with 'noble' and 'corruption' in the same sentence. But Dom knew that now Aless was talking he would be more relaxed and off guard, so prepared to discuss his demands again. Dom just had to be ready to capture his words. Not one for missing a trick, Dom took the chance of striking whilst the iron was hot.

Chapter 15: A Bundle of Cash

T he two men didn't hang around in the pool once their business had been discussed and they made their way back to the locker room. It was while they were getting dressed that Aless next surprised Dom.

"I gather by our chat the other day, Ben, that you and the missus are not together?"

"Yeah, that's right, we've been divorced for a while now. Why do you ask?"

"My cousin is about your age and she's looking for a fella. I thought I might be able to get you two together."

"No, you're all right, thanks. I have a girlfriend and don't think she will be too pleased with me running off with your cousin." Not sure Judy would like me describing her as a girlfriend, or understand it's just my cover story, thought Dom.

Dom still wondered what this conversation was about. Perhaps Aless likes me and wants me as family? Dom smiled at that thought, thinking of Judy.

Once dressed and reunited with his recording device, Dom offered to buy coffee in the lounge area. They settled down in a corner overlooking the tennis courts. Dom introduced the amount of cash Aless had asked for. Asking an indirect question Dom opened the conversation. "That's quite a bundle of cash, mate."

"Yeah, I always like to have a few bob round me. In my game you never know when you're going to need a few quid on the hurry-up. Don't worry, Ben, your wages are already taken care of. The important thing is that HP laptop, I need that. Once I've got that, the money and my passport I'm off. First Eurostar out of London and you won't see my arse for dust. How long are we looking at to get this stuff together?"

"This 'stuff' as you call it will never be referred to as to what it is from now on. The money we will call the 'paperwork'. The HP laptop we will call the 'box' and the passport the 'album.' The blue folder we'll call 'the book.' In that way, if anyone overhears us talking it will sound innocent."

"Yeah, good thinking, Ben. Paperwork, album, box, book, got it."

Dom didn't want to give the impression that this was going to be quick and easy. He wanted to build in time for the operational team to get their act together. "I'm going to bring Mark Turner back in on this. Don't worry, I'll cover his costs. The album and the box will be a piece of piss to get hold of, I can do that. I'm in and out of the property store all the time. It won't be difficult to slide your bits out with other items of property. The difficulty will be the paperwork. That amount of paper will be securely locked up. I'll get Mark to pull it for forensics or something. I'll work something out, leave it to me. Talking about paperwork, I'd like to see my paperwork now, Aless."

They finished their drinks and made their way to Aless's red Porsche.

"Get in, Ben, I've got something for you."

Dom found the passenger seat in a forward position and

found little wriggle room once he struggled to get in. Aless nodded at the glovebox. Dom gave him a quizzical look. Aless repeated the head movement, but this time raised his eyebrows at the glovebox.

Dom asked, "We're not going back to the silent treatment, are we?"

"No. Open the box, there's something for you in there."

Dom opened the box. Taking out a brown A4 size envelope, he looked inside. Dom saw bundles of twenty-pound notes with the bank bands wrapped round them. He knew that the bundles would consist of lots of one-thousand pounds. He quickly thumbed through them and counted ten individual bundles.

"That looks right to me, Aless. I'll trust you that there are a thousand quid in each, if not I know where you live. I'll be in touch, give me a few days to sort things out."

Both men laughed as Dom managed to extricate himself from the Porsche with the brown envelope tucked inside his jacket. Dom made his way back to his CID job motor as Aless drove off, followed by his personal police team in his wake. Once in the privacy of his car, Dom switched off the recording device and jabbed the air with a quick left, right, a one-two like a boxer in the ring. "Bish! Bosh! Left, right. It's in the can!"

Dom drove to the off-site for the debrief and to hand over his recording together with the ten thousand pounds. Paul was delighted with Dom's account of the meeting. Dom, relishing the moment, told them what Aless had said about his female cousin. "I reckon it was because he saw me naked," Dom said poker-faced. That invited a lot of laughter and piss taking at Dom's expense. Before leaving, it was agreed that once Paul had reviewed the recording and was satisfied he had the best evidence to convict Aless, Dom should call him and arrange the handover for Saturday morning in a public place. This was to be the arrest, or as the bosses say, the executive phase of the operation.

Chapter 16: Keystone Cops

The following day Dom received the green light from Daz to get the ball rolling for Saturday morning. He asked Dom to try to get Aless to agree to a hotel lounge for the handover, so they had Aless out in the open and not in his car. They wanted to minimise his potential escape routes and covertly deploy an arrest team on the day. Dom had no issues with these instructions and understood the boss's concern about the possibilities of a high-speed car chase across the city. Dom used an acronym to support this line of thinking: K.I.S.S. - Keep it simple stupid.

Dom got to work on his role the following day by calling Aless to tell him he had the album, the box and book safely under his control and Mark was doing his stuff around the paperwork. He was looking at doing the deal on Saturday morning as he was off duty this weekend. Dom suggested a hotel in the city centre. Aless said he'd give the location some thought, but Saturday morning would be fine. Dom was comfortable with Aless's response, so he agreed to call Aless on Friday to finalise the details.

Dom then called Daz and asked if the HP laptop, money and the passport could be available for the trade in case Aless asked for a flash of the goodies before going ahead with the exchange.

They both knew that wasn't unusual. Dom had previously used this 'flash money' tactic when buying kilos of drugs on the plot. In this case, it would signify Dom's professionalism in the eyes of Aless. Daz agreed it was a good idea and would speak with Mark to arrange it all.

Friday came round quickly, and Dom found himself sitting in his car calling Aless to finalise the detail for the following day. Aless sounded troubled.

"I want to meet in the Bristol Harbour Hotel by the riverside, Ben. I don't fancy that city centre place. I know people in there and I don't want anyone to see us."

Dom's thoughts began to work at double speed. Why has he changed the location? Has he just given me some old pony about knowing people at the hotel I suggested? What's the hotel he's suggesting? Will it be suitable for the operational team and the arrest phase? Dom decided he wasn't going to agree to this without the boss having the opportunity to give it the once over. Thinking over, Dom said, "Okay, Aless. I know the place you're on about. It's a bit posh, mate, it might not look right. What about another place?"

"What other place?"

Dom continued, "Leave it with me, Aless. I'll get back to you."

Dom called Daz and gave him the latest update. Within the hour, Daz was back on the phone giving Dom the thumbs up on Aless's suggested hotel. Daz pointed out to Dom that the hotel was close to Aless's penthouse apartment, not that it gave him nor the operational team any headache. Dom left further contact with Aless until later that evening. Just to break it up, Dom sent Aless a text agreeing to his choice of hotel and suggested they meet at one o'clock to do the deal. Aless responded by text confirming the location and the time. The final act of this saga was set.

Dom turned up as arranged at Daz's off-site office with his overnight bag on Friday afternoon. Daz had booked a couple of rooms in a low budget hotel about twenty miles away from the plot for Saturday's finale. Although Dom and Daz had double figures in years of experience in undercover work, they were not infallible and what Dom did next was a schoolboy error, to use Dom's words.

The two men booked into their hotel and Dom asked Daz to take him to the Bristol Harbour Hotel so he could have a look at the lounge and familiarise himself with the area. Nothing unusual for an undercover officer to research and reconnoitre the plot. The key is to do it without disturbing the environment, one of Dom's golden rules of undercover work – one rule he broke this time. Daz told Dom the operational team had booked a room on the top floor of the hotel to use as their command post. Dom wasn't over the moon with their choice, but he wasn't going to die in a ditch over it. On arrival at the hotel, Dom and Daz went to the hotel lounge area. After a short time, an attractive and flirty waitress approached and asked if they would like to order anything from the bar. Dom broke his golden rule. He engaged the flirty waitress in harmless banter. There were lots of chuckles and cheeky chat between the three of them. Daz and Dom finished their drinks and left, waving at the waitress with a mischievous wink as they departed.

The following morning, Daz and Dom revisited the Bristol Harbour Hotel. On arrival, they made their way to the command post on the top floor. On entering the room, Paul was surrounded by two op team members talking over the numbers needed for the arrest and control of Aless once he'd been nicked. Before the surveillance officers left the room, it was agreed that Dom would carry his jacket and place it on a seat next to him. When he stood to put on the jacket that was the trigger for the arresting officers to move in and effect the arrest quietly and with little fuss. Paul conducted the briefing during which he handed Aless's passport to Dom. It was inside a white envelope. The idea was to show Aless that Dom was serious. It was the equivalent of doing the 'flash money' on an undercover buy and it would keep Aless focused and convinced this was for real.

The next half an hour proved to be testing for Dom and his ability to think on his feet. Dom got the go ahead from Paul that everyone was in place, and it was over to him. Dom set up his recording device and called Aless from his burner phone. As Dom was talking to Aless, the house phone in the hotel room unexpectedly rang. Dom looked at the phone, then at Daz and Paul. He couldn't sound fazed or concerned about the interruption and carried on chatting to Aless. Daz moved across the room and picked up the house phone and listened, "Hello, sir, would you like brown or white bread with your tuna and cucumber sandwich?"

Daz looked across at Paul as he pressed the phone rocker switch to cut off the call. Paul mouthed, "Sorry," and held his head in his hands. Dom continued his chat.

"Where are you?" Aless asked.

"I'm at the hotel, mate," Dom said unhesitatingly.

"Great, I'm just round the corner, I'll be there pronto. See you there and we can get on with our business."

"Yeah, see you soon mate."

Dom put the phone down. "Shit, he's fucking here. I'll have

to get out of here. Fuck."

Cue a scene from the Keystone Cops. Dom grabbed his jacket and slipped the passport into the inside pocket. He activated his device and ran across the room and out of the door. Outside on the corridor he looked left and right. It all looked the same. He said in a low voice, "Which way to the lift?" But no one was there to answer. First, he went right. Wrong way. He spun round and ran by the command post door and turned right at the end of the corridor. He pressed the button requesting the lift. Then he thought. Fuck, what if Aless is already in the reception area and he sees me stepping out of the lift. Find the stairs, use the stairs.

The stairwell was just to the right of the lift and Dom pulled the door open and began to descend the concrete steps two at a time. After a few floors, he started arguing with himself whether it was jacket on or jacket off as the signal for the arrest team to close in and nick Aless. Fifty-Fifty. He decided to leave his jacket off and hoped he had guessed right. He wasn't counting the floors and found himself out of stairs and faced with an internal door. Not wanting to climb back up the stairs, he opened the door and stepped into some sort of beauty salon. He confidently said good day to a lady sitting reading a magazine and walked out of a door and onto the pavement. Taking a few minutes to get his bearings and breath back, he crossed the street and took up a position on the opposite pavement that gave him a view of the hotel main entrance. He was just in time to see Aless enter the hotel. Dom checked to ensure he still had the passport and device with him. Satisfied everything was present and correct, he slung his jacket over his shoulder, crossed the road and walked into the hotel reception with the grace of a swan on the outside but paddling like hell under water. He greeted Aless with a handshake. Aless hesitated.

Chapter 17: What Was All That About?

"Where have you just come from, Ben?"

Dom thought, Keep the lie as close to the truth as possible. "I was across the street waiting for you to arrive and satisfy myself it's not a set up and you're not working towards reporter of the year for some newspaper."

"I thought we'd moved on from there, Ben. Anyway, when you were on the phone before I heard another phone ring in the background, what was that all about?"

Thinking quickly, Dom pointed towards the reception desk where there were three or four phones on view, "I don't know, I was stood by the desk, so I guess it was one of them. What was it you just said about moving on?"

Respectful smiles were exchanged and Aless led the way into the lounge area.

What else can go wrong? Dom saw the flirty waitress was on duty. Dropping his head, Dom knew it was a pathetic gesture to protect him from recognition. Aless led the way to a quiet table in the corner. Dom ensured he took up the seat with his back to the room and placed his jacket on the vacant seat next to him. He had no view or control of the room, but because of his cock-up the day before it was his best shot at avoiding the waitress. Before they could get down to business, a male waiter asked if they would like anything from the bar. Aless asked for sparkling water with ice and Dom followed suit and made a mental note to thank God for sending the male waiter over. He wasn't out of the woods yet. Chatty Cathy, the waitress, was still a threat. The drinks arrived and as the waiter turned away from the table, Dom took the white envelope from his jacket pocket and placed it on the table in front of Aless.

"In there is the album, let's call it a sign of good will. Before we go further, I'd like to see the paperwork we agreed on. I don't see it here with you, mate, and that was the arrangement. What's the score?"

Aless shuffled in his seat and leaned across the table towards Dom.

"I didn't want to bring it in here, mate. I live round the corner, and I want to do it in the underground private car park, Ben."

Dom's brain changed up into top gear like a formula one racing car driver coming slowly out of a series of chicanes and looking down a long straight. He pressed the pedal and reacted. "Bollocks, Aless, you don't change the fucking plan on the day of the race. You stick to what we agreed. So, get home and get your fucking money and bring it in here. Don't fuck me about now or I'm out of here and you're going to jail." Dom knew that the surveillance team couldn't cover the exchange and the arrest in an underground car park. By taking a strong aggressive stance with Aless he bought himself some more thinking time.

"Ben, calm down, mate. The money is there, mate, all of it. Just bring the paper, box, and book, mate. What's the difference here or there?"

"I'll tell you what the fucking difference is. I turn up there

77

with the stuff and you get your muscle to rob me. What the fuck do I do then, call the police?"

"Ben, I'll go and get the money. I'll put it on the front seat of my car. I'll drive by and you can see the papers there and we can meet up in the car park and do the deal. It's as simple as that."

"I've told you, Aless. We don't change the plan at the last minute. I'm going to pay the bill and you and I are going for a walk and a chat to sort this out. I'll be back in a minute."

Dom stood. He picked up the white envelope and his mobile phone and put on his jacket. He turned away and made his way to the bar to pay the bill. When he turned back towards the table, he saw the waiter clearing away the glasses from an empty table.

Dom went out into the reception and pressed the button for the lift. He'd had enough of the stairs. Back on the top floor, Paul opened the door to the command post and let Dom in. He apologised to Dom for his earlier cock-up and shook his hand, thanking him for his work. Dom told Paul the issue of the money and the underground car park and that he'd made the decision to call the arrest team in. They both knew if the money was at his penthouse flat, it would be found and seized in the subsequent house search. Dom debriefed Paul and handed over his exhibits and went down for a bite to eat before setting off home to see his lad. He said his farewells to Daz as they travelled down in the lift. Both men knew they would meet again soon.

Walking into the lounge area he made eye contact with Chatty Cathy. Dom sat himself at a table and asked her for a menu. She smiled at Dom and in a West Country accent said, "That was a little bit different earlier on," as she turned towards the table Dom and Aless had occupied a little earlier.

Looking blank, Dom said, "Sorry, what was different?"

Still smiling, Cathy took Dom's order for the house burger and coke. Dom sat enjoying his own company and reflecting on the day. He thought, You couldn't make this stuff up.

Chapter 18: Heroin

W hat was it Bob Geldof's band sang? '*I don't like Mondays.*' Well, let me tell you Sundays are not the best day of the week to buy heroin in East London, especially if it's a set up.

Dom knew a good lad, we can call him Macca for the purpose of this job. Dom worked with Macca on the Regional, he was a UCO who had been dragged into a drugs buy of heroin in the London area. It was common for a UCO to be pulled into jobs like that. Dom and Macca had built up a good, healthy, and trusted working relationship. Macca had many assets, including having a motorcycle licence. He was a great rider and could handle his powerful 1200cc BMW like Carl Fogarty going round Donnington Park.

Macca was short, standing at five foot five. He'd never have met the minimum height requirement when Dom first joined the job but once that was abolished, Macca joined up. He had a mass of unruly blond hair. Once, while they were attending a debrief after a long day on a dead surveillance plot, Dom got a shout to get back to the office on the hurry up. He left the comfort and safety of his four door, two litre tin can, call sign Hotel 9, and accepted Macca's offer of a speedy return to the office. This was the first and the last time Dom got on a motorcycle with anyone. Macca took every millimetre of slack out of Dom's underpants. It was a terror ride; Dom was sure they flew past a few landmarks and points of interest, but his eyes were tight shut from start to finish. His parting words to the laughing Macca in the rear yard of the RCS office were, "You're fucking mental, mate, mental. Thanks for the once in a lifetime never to be repeated experience." Dom tossed, more like threw, the crash helmet Macca had given him back at him.

Regaining composure, Dom adjusted his clothing below the waistline and made his way to the boss's office to hear why the terrifying journey was necessary. It was another job that was in the planning stage and the DCI, Eamonn O'Donnell together with his second in command, the 2 I/C, DI Barry Bowen wanted to see what Dom's thoughts were on a deployment.

As they finished the planning and development stage, Macca knocked on the office door and stuck his still smiling face through the opening. He excused himself and asked if he could have five minutes. That's how it was on the RCS, you could take a lead with anyone whether they had rank or not. However, working relationships were always professional and respectful apart from the usual banter, and that was also a form of respect and togetherness.

Eamonn looked over his glasses. "What do you want, you ugly midget?"

Macca replied, "Nice to see you too, boss. I've just had a phone call on that heroin job. They want a meeting and I'll need to move the job on to someone further up the food chain. I was thinking of pulling you on to it, Dom, if you fancy it, with your blessing, boss."

Eamonn turned to Dom. "Do you want to work with this munchkin?"

Barry chipped in, "That's an insult to munchkins."

Macca came back in a blink of an eye, "All right, all right. I've got feelings and emotions you know. I'm going to the Fed (Police Federation) about you lot."

"Okay with me, boss," Dom said.

"And it's okay with me. Take care out there, fellas. Those streets aren't safe. Good luck," Eamonn said.

Before Macca and Dom left the office holding hands like two four-year-olds out on a school trip, Macca said, sounding like a four-year-old, "Thank you Mr O'Donnell, thank you Mr Bowen."

Eamonn, despite laughing, managed to say, "Get the fuck out of here, you two. God help us if this is our best."

Macca and Dom went into the kitchen and made their own drinks. Macca had been in the office for a year or so before Dom first arrived. On Dom's first day he offered to make him a brew – never again. Macca was a coffee man and Dom fancied a tea for a change. Dom watched him that first day as he put the tea bag, boiling water, and the milk in the cup, all at the same time. From that moment on, Dom would vent on the subject, "Any proper tea connoisseur will tell you that the tea bag is scientifically designed to diffuse in boiling water. As soon as you add the milk it destroys that process. That's why they can't make proper tea in Europe; the water is never boiling. The other cardinal sin is to have the tea bag in the cup together with the milk. No. The tea bag and the milk should be like polar bears and penguins. They never meet."

Anyway, they took their hot drinks into the empty main office as the rest of the team were still making their sedate way back from the shit day on the plot. Macca gave Dom the run down on the job. He was dealing with a Pakistani guy by the name of Abdul, who was working for the supplier who was also a Pakistani. Another UCO had introduced Abdul to Macca but that other UCO's involvement in the operation would disappear if it came to a court case, owing to public interest immunity issues. That would result in Macca being the first UCO to be able to give evidence in any case involving Abdul. Macca told Dom that Abdul wouldn't make any decisions. He always had to check out everything with his boss and get back to him.

"Well, mate that's not a bad thing, plays into our hands," Dom said. "What you are calling yourself and what's our connection?"

Macca said, "He knows me as Sonny, and you are the money man flying down from Manchester. You're called Stan, as in Stan Ogden out of Corrie years ago."

Dom stopped sipping his tea. "You are kidding me, Macca, fucking Stan, I don't think I look like a Stan."

"Yeah, you do. Stan the man that can. One last thing, it looks like the meeting will probably be on for this Sunday."

"You are joking, Macca, Sunday? I've arranged a trip to the coast with Judy and the kids this weekend to make up for letting them down last weekend, no way is she going to let this happen."

Just as Dom finished, he heard an unfamiliar ring tone coming from Macca's leather jacket. Macca took the phone out and looking at the screen he said, tilting his head to one side, "Fuck me! That's spooky, it's Abdul. I'll let it go to answer phone, see what he wants." After a minute his phone gave out two beeps. "There he is, left a message, let's see what he's got to say." Macca punched in a PIN code and put the phone to his ear. As he listened to the message, he kept looking at Dom then smiled as he put the phone down. "Looks like we're going for a briefing, Stan, and get you signed up to this job. We're on for Sunday. His man wants to meet my man and that's you."

"Shit, Macca, I'm dead. Judy will go ballistic. I'll put a call in to her." Dom took his mobile from his pocket and pulled Judy up from his latest call list. "Hi baby, are you all right to talk?"

"Hang on a tick, let me just move away. Yeah, okay, darling. What's going on? I thought you were on a surveillance today?" Judy said.

Dom explained the dead plot and the motorbike ride with Macca. "Judy, I'm going to be late home tonight, I've got a briefing in North London this evening..." *Bite the bullet, Dom, just tell her,* he thought, "...for a job on Sunday."

Judy went off on one and reminded Dom of his promises from last week. In fact, she could have compiled a best seller on the let downs over the years.

"Come on, Judy, that's not right. You of all people know how it is." Dom didn't think she heard anything he was saying. He was getting both barrels followed by a quick reload and both barrels again. "Judy, calm down for crying out loud, I will make it up to you and the kids." But before he'd finished the sentence the phone went dead. Returning his phone to his pocket, Dom gave Macca a whimsical smile. "Thanks for that, mate. Let's go and get briefed up."

Turning to walk out of the office, Dom heard Macca call out, "Do you want a lift on the back of the bike? It will be quicker."

Without turning, Dom held the index finger on his right hand in the air, went to the rear yard and jumped into the spare car affectionately known as the 'skip' and set off to another RCS office, the one that had ownership of the heroin buy. There, Dom would get 'sworn in' (signed up by the SIO) to the job followed by a meeting with the cover officer to discuss strategy and the deployment details. He got home at around nine o'clock that evening. A polar bear or a penguin would have felt more at home as he walked through the door with a forced, "Hi, baby. I'm home." It was frosty.

It was only Wednesday night. Dom had three days before the job to fire up the emotional central heating and get Judy to understand and believe he had no choice. Problem being she knew the ropes. He did have a choice, he could have made his excuses and walked away from the job because he had a trip to the seaside planned. But this was part of his job. Dom made his way into the kitchen and took the bottle of Jameson out of the cupboard, filled a tall glass with ice cubes and poured a large one. "Do you want a drink, Judy?" The silence was deafening so Dom tried, "I'll fix you a vodka and tonic, babe."

"Don't bother, I'm going up to bed in a minute. If you're up and away early in the morning sleep in the spare room if you don't mind." More frost.

Oh, piss off, 'if you don't mind,' Dom thought. Instead, he said, "Yeah, okay, we're back on that surveillance, so I'll use the spare room, don't want to spoil your beauty sleep, do we? Not that you need it, darling." Judy loved Dom's sense of humour, and he used it often to win her back around just like John Wayne used a six gun. He switched on the TV in the kitchen and sat on the work surface, nursing his long Jameson over ice in one hand and catching up on the Sky Sports app on his phone with the other.

'Bing' – an incoming WhatsApp message from Judy. *She really isn't speaking to me*, Dom thought. He opened the message:

Ice, slice of orange and Aperol in my vodka and tonic you bastard and I want table service.

Dom felt a prickly heat rising but followed the instructions to the letter. Serving up her drink, he said, "Sorry about the trip to the coast, I'd agreed to do the job before anyone knew it was going on the pavement on the weekend. Macca asked me then the call came in from the target and, well, you know the rest."

Judy said, "Don't worry." No more she said.

Chapter 19: Brown Wallet

On the Sunday afternoon, Dom picked up Macca up from his home in his covert car. No crazy motorbike ride today. The only other bit of covert stuff he had with him was his brown wallet containing his covert driving licence, bank cards, about three hundred pounds of the Chief Constable's dosh and a few bits and pieces you would expect to find in any guy's wallet. They drove across to the outskirts of Dagenham and met with their cover officer, Graham. He gave them recording devices and tapes and wished them luck. "I'll be on the end of the phone, boys, got a family do on this afternoon. You're not expecting any grief, are you Macca?"

Bloody hell, I hope this never gets back to Judy, Dom thought. Back in the day they sometimes flew by the seat of their pants. Dom knew Graham would be on the end of a phone and sober as he never touched a drop of alcohol. Macca was comfortable with the arrangements which meant Dom was too. Dom also knew he and the munchkin were old enough and ugly enough to look after themselves to a certain degree. This method of 'covering a deployment' was common practice with some outfits. It was a good learning exercise for Dom in his later undercover life when he was covering a job. He made sure he would always be close on hand if his UCOs needed him. It was not always necessary to have a team around if it was just a meeting in the development phase of an operation. When the stakes were increased the manpower level moved up with it. *So, no big shakes deploying with nothing around to dig you out if needed*, Dom mused.

Macca and Dom made their way to the meeting venue, a retail park in Dagenham. They sat in a coffee lounge until it closed and then in Dom's car, waiting for Abdul to call as he was supposed to call and vector them on to the meet. It was now an hour after the agreed time and getting dark. Macca, aka Sonny, had left two messages on the target's phone. Macca and Dom agreed to give it twenty more minutes and then fuck off, leaving a message on Abdul's phone letting him know they had pissed off because he hadn't shown. Just as time was about up, Sonny's phone rang. He activated his recording device and answered the phone. Sonny expressed his disappointment in having to hang around and that Stan was about to go back to Manchester and the deal was off. It was high risk on Sonny's behalf, but they had to be real and if this guy was serious about supplying two kilos of heroin, he had to do this without any pressure from them. They could show enthusiasm but not drive the job. They didn't want to cross the line and give a defence team a legal 'Agent Provocateur' argument. Abdul directed them to Barking train station and said he would meet them there in an hour. *Okay, game on again and Abdul is still driving the job*, Dom thought.

Barking station was quiet, nothing like it is Monday to Friday with hundreds of workers packed onto the trains heading for the city. Sonny had grabbed a couple of the Sundays and Dom read the sports pages while Sonny interrupted his concentration with clues from the crossword he was struggling with. "Four down, postman's round?"

After a pregnant pause, Dom took the bait. "How many letters?"

"Fucking thousands. The old ones are the best, I'm here all week," Sonny said with one of those laughs that sounds like an excited pig under a truffle tree.

Time was marching on again and they had to look real. If they were real, would they hang about and get the run around from Abdul? Sonny and Dom, aka Stan, debated the possibilities and gave Graham a ring to get his take on things. He in turn called the SIO to get his decision and policy on their next move. It was decided to wait for half an hour and text Abdul to say they were off.

Half an hour slowly ticked by, and Sonny activated his recorder and called Abdul to give him the news. Abdul gave some moody excuse about one of his kids being ill and was very apologetic and almost begged them not to go. He asked if they could get to East Ham to make life a bit easier for him. Sonny, buying time, told Abdul he would have a chat with Stan and call him back. That was a good move as this allowed them to pass the ball to their cover officer and the SIO.

It's the SIO who must justify such decisions to a judge in the event the thing goes to trial. In this case, Sonny and Stan had told Abdul they were out, but then he pleaded for them to stay in the game. That would be the justification given by the SIO.

Macca called him back and agreed they would make their way to East Ham. It was now about ten o'clock at night and they had been pulled around for the last few hours. Macca and Dom arrived at Micky Ds and grabbed more coffee and tea. Dom reflected he should have gone for a hot chocolate because the tea was crap. They sat outside on one of those tables that have

89

benches fixed to the table, so you must climb over with one leg like getting on a horse. In those days, Dom had a liking for a 'la-di-da' (Cockney rhyming slang for cigar). He had one in his jacket ready to smoke on his drive home. Once home, he used the cigars as a companion to his beloved Jameson to ease the stresses of work. Dom decided it was time for a smoke and took out the Villiger cigar out and lit it, taking in a lung full of the smoke. As he was enjoying that moment when you exhale the smoke, Macca tapped his foot under the table and nodded towards a car that had just pulled into the car park. Macca said, "I don't believe it. He's just turned up." They both activated their recording devices and put on their game face.

"Abdul, mate, this is Stan and he's pissed off. He wanted to walk away hours ago, what the fuck is going on?"

Before Abdul could reply, Dom said, "Leave it out, Sonny. I'll speak for myself. I tell you this, Abdul, I don't hang around for any man. I'm not really bothered if we do this bit of work. I want you to tell your boss that I'm not some two bob Northerner who gets dragged about fucking London on a Sunday evening to sit outside a fucking Micky Ds. Now unless you have some good news for me, you can shove your gear up your arse." It was his turn to adopt a high-risk strategy. They had to look, act, and speak real. Had they given the appearance of weak and desperate criminals, they would run the risk of setting themselves up for a rip off on the day of the trade.

Abdul threw out his arms by his side with palms open. Dom interpreted that as a sign of a deep apology, confirmed when he said, "Sorry. My boss too. It is my fault, not him. I had an illness in the family. I'm so sorry. Come, sit in my car and we talk. We do business."

On hearing the invitation, Dom sensed a red warning light.

He was sure Macca did too. It's not a good idea to get into a car you have no control over. But they got in. Dom sat with the door held open with his foot and filled the inside of the car with thick cigar smoke. Perhaps Abdul hadn't noticed the open door, but he began to drive.

"What the fuck are you doing?" Dom shouted and pulled the door shut in fear of falling out. Macca was in the back. Dom glanced over his shoulder and made eye contact with him.

Abdul was gibbering away in broken, heavily accented English. Dom's brain was working at warp speed. *We have lost control and are being driven away to an unknown destination.* "Where the fuck are we going, Abdul?" Dom demanded.

In broken English, he said, "I take you... to... house... see... friend. He... explain... apologise."

This was bad. Both UCOs thought, *No way are we walking into a house with recording devices on us. Unknown premises, no one outside the car knows where we are. Big no, no, red light, got to stop this happening and fast.* Once again, Dom glanced at Macca. *A few hours ago, he was cracking shit one liners doing the crossword, now we are in a bad guy's car being driven across London. And neither of us are laughing. Think, Dom, you've got to get out of this car.*

Looking ahead, Dom saw a BP petrol station illuminated like Blackpool Tower. He thought, *It's well lit. It will have CCTV and an attendant with an eyeball on the forecourt.* "Pull into that petrol station, Abdul. We need to have a fucking chat," Dom said. There was not a please or thank you. It was an order with no room for negotiation.

He complied with Dom's demand and pulled over by the water and air area. Dom turned to Macca, "Mate, just get out for a minute. I'm having a chat with this guy." This was a double-edged strategy. Firstly, if Abdul was to drive off again, Macca could call in the cavalry and get the car index, giving Dom a fighting chance of survival. Dom also thought it would give Abdul the impression he did not want to belittle him in front of the guy he thought was Sonny.

Once Macca was outside the car, Dom took control. "Right, Abdul get this. We are not going to anyone's house. You can bring your 'friend' boss to a meeting with me tomorrow at two o'clock at the 'Blind Beggar' pub. I'm from Manchester, I know where it is, so you and your 'friend' should have no problem finding it. Now I'm getting out of this car, and you can get back to your boss, give him my regards and best wishes and I look forward to seeing him tomorrow. Tell him to have the two keys [kilos] ready to go and we'll have the money. We can have a chat and agree how we're going to do the trade and get on with it. You know how to get in touch with us. Good night."

With that, Dom got out of the car and joined Macca by the air hose. Abdul drove off into the distance. Dom then noticed the attendant waving frantically at them. *Now what?* he thought. Then he realised he still had a lit cigar in his hand. Dom waved back and walked off the forecourt towards a mini cab office opposite.

Macca and Dom exchanged a few comments about the last ten minutes, before Dom said, "Shit, my recorder is still running." *Some stuff for the operational team to PII out,* he thought.

They took a mini cab back to Micky Ds and jumped into Dom's car. Macca called Graham to update him about the events since they had last spoken and the arrangements for the following day. They later met up with Graham and a DI from the operational team to complete their notes, debrief and hand over the recordings as exhibits. It was agreed to meet at The

Tower Bridge Hotel at midday the following day.

Dom dropped off Macca at his house and then had an additional hour or so drive back to his place. He got home at around two in the morning. First, a small Jameson and then he snuggled down with Judy who didn't move a muscle. "Night, night," Dom said, kissing her head gently.

She muttered, "How the job go, baby?"

Dom's head was now on the pillow as he said, "Yeah, okay baby. Back on it tomorrow." Judy didn't need to know how close Dom and Macca were to being kidnapped. Sometimes, a need-to-know policy is required, and Judy didn't need to know.

Six hours later Dom was back in the car heading for Macca. On the way to the briefing hotel, they recalled the events of the previous night. Macca congratulated Dom on his quick thinking and then took the piss out of him for using the 'Blind Beggar' as a meeting location.

Dom went on the defensive. "To be honest, mate, it was the only landmark I could think of under the circumstances. Driving home last night I realised that they are probably Muslims and might have an issue coming into a pub, but we can deal with that over the phone if it's a problem."

They arrived at the briefing location and made their way to a hotel room on the third floor. Graham opened the door. Both UCOs walked into the room to be met by the SIO, Pat, the DI from the undercover office, and two men Dom didn't recognise. Macca and Dom sat on the end of the double bed. The other members of the group were seated on chairs, the windowsill and the corner of the desk.

Pat introduced the two unknown officers as belonging to

the Professional Standards Department (PSD). They were both Detective Inspectors, but their names didn't mean a thing to Dom. When he heard PSD, he thought, *I'm in the shit.*

Pat must have seen or sensed Dom's concern as he said, "Nothing for you two to fret about." He then took them through the events of yesterday and the timeline. Macca and Dom confirmed everything as correct, eager to find out why these guys from PSD were here. Pat spoke again. "Okay, lads. The reason you guys were getting dragged about yesterday is because Abdul is a registered snout [Informant] to a Detective Sergeant on the South London Drug Squad. That DS is setting this job up. PSD dropped on to the DS recently and have had his and Abdul's phones hooked up [telephone tap] for the last few days. Macca, your burner phone has been double busy on the tap over the last few days and cell site analysis had you in East London yesterday in the company of Abdul's phone. With me so far, fellas?"

Macca and Dom looked at each other. "Yeah..." Macca said, "pray do continue."

Pat continued, "They had Abdul chatting away on the line, talking about a trade at the Blind Beggar later today. The reason Abdul was late getting anywhere yesterday was he was waiting for instructions and direction from the Drug Squad DS. You may have had your plan on how this deal was going down, but the bent DS had other ideas. Abdul wasn't going to be there; he was going to have some moody reason to give to his 'friend' on why he had to leave to fight another day. Once you two, the suppliers, the money and the gear were on the pavement, the bent DS with his team were going to call a strike and nick you all. Drugs, money and a high body count in the bag. The Drug Squad team would be dining out on their success and the kudos that goes with it."

Dom thought, *Shit...this is a perfect example of the concept of Agent Provocateur or state generated crime.*

Macca and Dom were stood down and the PSD took over the gig. Dom did suggest that Macca and he were happy to continue the buy to secure best evidence, but Dick and Dan from the PSD had their game plan, and it didn't include Sonny and Stan. Dom learned later that there were protocols in place to avoid a blue-on-blue situation. This job was an example that they worked in that two deployments involving the same target resulted in one operation taking precedence over the other.

Dom got home much earlier than expected. He walked in and announced his presence with his usual, "Hi, baby I'm home."

Judy appeared in the hallway with an inquisitive expression. "Why are you back so early? What went wrong?"

Grinning at her sharp perception, he said, "Let's grab a drink, 'cause for sure I could do with a long one. V and T with all the extras, darling?"

The emotional central heating had returned to normal. "Make it a large one, babe." By the time they had sat down in the lounge, and Dom recounted his adventure over the last twenty-four-hour period, he thought of the bent DS sat in his police cell on a Monday evening with Bob Geldof playing in his head, '*I don't like Mondays.*'

Chapter 20: Northeast Lorry Job

Dominic gained several skills that were of use to him as an undercover officer. During his military service he obtained three driving licences. The first was the standard driving licence. He did this in a military Land Rover at the age of eighteen. It was common practice back in the day for unlicenced squadron members to take a vehicle for a '*cabby,*' a short unsupervised drive, around the motor transport yard. The yard circuit was two long straights connected with tight turns at each end. Imagine charioteers in the *Ben Hur* film careering around Circus Maximus in ancient Rome.

The yard was always busy with vehicles manoeuvring and soldiers moving around the place. On one of Dom's early illegal 'cabby' exploits, he crashed into a stationary one-ton trailer which in turn smashed into a metal corrugated wall which collapsed and brought down some of the asbestos roof panels of a garage. The racket must have attracted the attention of everyone within a five-mile radius, including the transport sergeant. Dom got out of the Land Rover and assessed the damage to the building and the vehicle. Thinking he might get away unnoticed, he quickly swept away the broken headlight glass with his boot and pulled the crushed wing away from the front tyre. As he was about to make off from the scene of the crime, the transport sergeant bellowed in a thick Northern Irish accent.

"Where the fuck do you think you're going, sonny? Come here." Naturally for a soldier, Dom made his way across to the sergeant who was built like the proverbial brick toilet. "How on God's earth did you manage to do that, boy?" he asked.

Dom, never short of an answer, said, "I think oversteer, Sarge."

The big Irishman wasn't impressed with Dom's flippant reply. "Oversteer? How long have you had a licence?"

"That's the problem, Sarge, I don't have one."

That was an early introduction to completing paperwork in triplicate, a skill that wasn't lost in his police career or the following encounter with the military justice system when he was disciplined by the Officer Commanding, OC, Orders which is the military equivalent to appearing at the civilian Magistrates' Courts.

Suitably punished by the OC, Dom was placed on the next basic driving course. The other two driving qualifications he gained were a Class Three Heavy Goods Vehicle, HGV or LGV, and a Track Licence (Group H) which qualified him to drive armoured fighting vehicles, AFVs, such as a tank! You may think that was a high-risk strategy by Her Majesty's Armed Forces considering his early driving record.

But it was the HGV licence Dom used on several deployments as an undercover officer. Years after obtaining his class three, he passed an HGV class one course and moved on to bigger and heavier lorries. Dom spent a lot of time improving his lorry driving skills. He would take himself off driving for a haulage company doing real haulage work for a week every two or three months. He knew this was the best way to be able to talk the talk and walk the walk when deployed infiltrating an organised crime group, OCG, that was looking for transport to convey drugs from Europe into the United Kingdom. Other OCGs may be looking to carry out staged lorry hijackings or theft of a high value loads with a compliant driver or haulier, and tragically, people smuggling. Irrespective of the illegal load, an OCG needs a skilful, experienced and road smart driver. Dom eventually ticked all those boxes.

On one deployment, Dom was inserted into a conspiracy to steal a lorry load of branded spirits. Andy, another UCO, was already embedded into the OCG. He had more than a bit of a reputation within the undercover world, revelling in the name of the Crafty Cockney. Dom described him as a protected species because of his close friendship and historical connections with a member of the undercover office cover team in his force. Andy and the cover officer had served on a unit where several of the team had been discredited and shown to be bent, corrupt, by an investigative journalist, and featured in a BBC TV programme. Andy and the cover officer came out of the enquiry without a glove landing on them but both men had a bad smell around them for some time. Andy didn't even have a background in haulage, but because of his protected status and his mate he turned up on various jobs around the country, and the Newcastle job was one of them.

The operational team based in the Northeast were experienced in this type of operation, having Scottish and Newcastle Brewery on their doorstep. They were led by DI Terry White, a seasoned career detective, who was just coming up for his retirement but still had the same enthusiasm as the youngest guy on his team. He had balls of steel and wasn't risk averse. It was not until Dom arrived in the Northeast and spoke to Bob

CHAPTER 20: NORTHEAST LORRY JOB

from the undercover unit that he got the story behind Andy being on the plot.

About six months previously, Andy had been deployed into a city centre bar frequented by several criminals associated with a core nominal who was supplying and importing class 'A' drugs, namely cocaine. Andy and Tracey, a female UCO from Bob's team, were authorised to purchase personal amounts of drugs and infiltrate the supply chain with the operational aim of getting to Mister Big. Andy would fly up from London on a Thursday evening for a couple of days every two or three weeks with the excuse of visiting his girlfriend, Tracey.

Andy had managed to identify a couple of street dealers but had not got close to the next rung up the ladder. Tracey wasn't enjoying working with him. He was always going off on his own during the day without telling Tracey where he was going. If she asked, he would tell her he was off for a mooch round the town or to the local gym. The DI, Terry White, had an uncomfortable feeling about him and wasn't over impressed with Andy's expenses – flights and hire cars plus his spending over the bar and in restaurants, not to mention the gym membership fee. Terry saw it as a bit of a piss-take and was going to pull the plug until Andy came up with some valuable info on one of the main targets. Andy's contact had said he was looking for a haulier who had a contract with Scottish and Newcastle and fancied a tax-free payday for losing a forty-footer, a trailer, full of branded spirits. Andy had seen an opportunity to enhance his status with the OCG and suggested he might know someone and left it there. In fairness to Andy, that was a good bit of work. He didn't make a promise he couldn't deliver on and gave the operational team the option to go with it or not. It gave Andy a stay of execution as far as the DI and team were concerned.

Dom was then brought in and instructed to go into the pub with Andy and get introduced to the target. The team had done the background on this gadgie called Chris. Gadgie is Newcastle and Glasgow slang for a no-mark or low-life. The intelligence reports on Chris revealed he was the real deal, well connected, with full criminal pedigree and well in with the core nominal. They wanted Dom to sound out Chris and the prospect of progressing the job. That was the official brief. But off the record, Bob wanted Dom to find out what Andy got up to in the town.

Dom told Bob that he needed to run things by Kath, his boss, and suggested Terry gave his gaffer a bell to explain the concerns around Andy and if she was okay with it. She wasn't totally comfortable with the off the record chat with Bob, but she agreed, subject to her boss giving his blessing to the job. It wasn't the first time that Dom and Kath had heard that someone had questioned Andy's methods, performance, and expenses. That possibly outweighed her reservations. They knew Andy planned to fly up from London the next day and had been told that Dom would be there for the briefing, and a chat on how to introduce Dom to Chris as a haulier with a contract with Scottish and Newcastle for one of the big supermarkets.

After Dom's meeting with Bob, he set off for the hotel he'd booked online using his booking.com account in his pseudonym. He gave Kath a call to give her the heads-up on the job and time to think over the Andy issue. Dom arrived at the Little Haven Hotel in South Shields, a hotel he had used before when he was doing witness protection work. He knew there was no chance of him bumping into anyone he would be infiltrating over the next few days.

The hotel is set on the banks of the River Tyne, surrounded by sandy beaches and grassland, just a few miles from Newcastle city centre. Dom thought that the hotel and surroundings would not look out of place in a Miami holiday brochure. As he pulled into the car park, Kath called him to inform him she had spoken with Terry and was happy with everything, and the paperwork was being sent down in the morning. *All good*, he thought, so made his way to the reception. The receptionist asked him if he had stayed with them before and without hesitation he said, "No, first time." Dom *had* stayed there previously but he had used a different name in his witness protection role. Had he said 'yes,' the receptionist would have punched *the* name into the hotel booking system and would have expected Dominic's details to appear. The negative answer avoided a full interrogation by the receptionist in completing the booking in procedure.

After a long day he settled into his hotel room with his mate, a bottle of Jameson whiskey, together with the crossword and the sudoku in the daily newspaper. He was sound asleep within minutes.

Chapter 21: The DFDS Ferry

The following morning, he woke fully rested and ready for the day. He jumped out of bed like a five-year-old on Christmas morning and pulled the curtains open. Luckily, he had slept in his shorts. As he pulled the curtains apart, a DFDS Ferry from Amsterdam heading for Newcastle was passing within what appeared to be feet from his window. Dom could see into the ferry windows and watched passengers eating breakfast. He saw others dressing in their cabins. No doubt they had an unobstructed view of Dom dressed only in his black Adidas shorts. He smiled and waved at anyone who might be watching.

After a full English breakfast, he jumped into his Mercedes E-Class and made his way towards Bob's office. On the way, Dom called into an old mate from his military days. Scotty and his wife Dora had settled in the area after the end of Scotty's military career. Dom wanted to give Scotty the heads-up he would be in and around the city for a few days. Scotty had joined up with Dom in the seventies and retired as a Major after forty years of service. He had served in many trouble spots around the globe and had an impressive chest of medals. He had that many, Dom joked that Scotty would have a little man walk behind him on parade wearing some of his medals.

Scotty and Dora greeted Dom like the old friend he was and spent an hour pulling up sandbags and swinging the lamp about their antics from yesteryear. Scotty and Dora knew what Dom's day job was and how challenging and dangerous it could be. Dom vaguely outlined what he was doing in town and how to behave if he or Dora happened to see or bump into him over the next few days around the Toon, as the city of Newcastle is known by Geordies. Probably not much chance but on a previous visit to the city, Dom and another undercover officer on a different job crossed paths in a hotel car park. As per normal protocol, the UCOs ignored each other and had a chat later about their encounter. Scotty assured Dom that he and Dora wouldn't be around the city centre that weekend as he was on painting and decorating duty. Scotty walked Dom back to his car, embracing with a real man hug which lingered for a while, a sign of the respect and bond between the two men. As Dom drove off, he saw Dora and Scotty in his rear-view mirror waving farewell. Within seconds, he was back focused on the task in hand.

The drive to Bob's office in the north of the city took Dom through the Tyne Tunnel, a journey of about a mile under the Tyne River. As he emerged from the sodium lighting and into the natural light he was in the heart of the city, heading north towards Ponteland and a meeting with Andy and Bob. On the way, Bob called him and asked Dom to make for the Double Tree Hotel close to the airport where he and Terry would meet Dom in the lounge area for a chat.

Dom walked into the hotel and made his way to the lounge. Bob and the boss were sitting in the corner, side by side with their backs to the wall, giving them a panoramic view of the lounge area and anyone entering the hotel. Dom wasn't looking forward to having his back to the room. As he approached the two men, Terry stood then greeted Dom and excused himself for a quick visit to the loo. Dom took Terry's seat next to Bob and wasn't going to be moved.

The meeting was arranged at the Double Tree hotel as it was close to the airport and Andy was flying up from down south, arriving at six-fifty that evening. On arrival, he would collect a hire car from Avis and drive to the hotel for a briefing. A room at the hotel had been booked for three nights under Bob's covert company name. As well as serving as a secure briefing and debriefing location, the room was made available to Dom for the duration of his stay. Tracey had a flat in the city centre that went with her alter ego, her legend. Her cover story was that she worked for a high-end events company that provided services for overseas clients in the UK and worldwide. This gave her a reason why she wasn't local all the time. Like all undercover officers, Tracey had a life outside the police and needed time to live it. To fit their legend of boyfriend and girlfriend, Andy stayed in Tracey's flat on his visits, using one of the two spare rooms.

Once Terry came back from the loo, Dom shared his thoughts about his idea of a cover story. He was thinking of purporting to be a haulier who was having a cashflow problem and needed a quick cash injection to settle a VAT bill. He was going to portray himself as a novice at wrongdoing and show he was anxious if he should get caught, in the process losing his business and going to jail. Dom carried on telling them he and Andy would come up with a story and background on how they know each other. Dom was already thinking which UCO he would use as the driver on the day if the job progressed. After an exchange of ideas and small talk, the three men went their separate ways.

Prior to leaving, Bob handed Dom the key card to his room on the third floor. Terry and Bob told Dom they would be back at seven o'clock that evening to brief him, Tracey, and Andy. Dom went out into the car park to get his case from his car, then picked up a complimentary newspaper on the way to his spacious room on the third floor.

On arriving at his room Dom hung the 'do not disturb' sign on the outside of the door handle, the usual routine for him. When leaving his room, he always left the television on loud enough to be heard from the corridor, but not to be an annoyance to people in the adjoining rooms. The 'do not disturb' sign stayed on the door handle. Dom believed this gave the impression the room was occupied. The next task was to get his phones on charge. He would often have a handful of phones with him depending on his operational commitments. He always had his job phone, supplied by his force and known to police colleagues, his wife and kids, friends and neighbours. Then he had his covert phone in his long-term pseudonym or legend name. This phone was used by people and companies that knew him as Dom wanted them to know him. No contacts who knew this number knew Dom was an undercover cop. In addition, he had burner phones he was using on other jobs. These roles may be just walk on and walk off jobs or a supporting role for a colleague deployed on a long-term deployment.

So, all phones were checked and charged. He placed them on 'vibrate on silent.' There was nothing worse than talking to a target on the phone and one or two of the other phones rang. Dom had a couple of hours to fill before his meeting at seven. He put the television on and lay back on the bed, watching a disaster movie about a comet on track to smash into Earth. He never saw the end of the world having slipped into a deep sleep.

Dom thought about his wardrobe for this first night on the plot. He knew Andy's style, always flash and designer gear. Dom usually had a more mature style, giving the impression of a successful understated middle-aged man. Adapting his style to look like a haulier wouldn't be too difficult a task. Just before seven, Bob called Dom to tell him he, Terry and Tracey were on their way up. The three arrived at the room separately at least a couple of minutes apart from each other. Bob told Dom that Andy's flight was on time and he would be with them shortly. Whilst they were waiting, Dom was signed up for the job and issued with a PNB and a burner phone. He put the relevant numbers into the phone and familiarised himself with the settings, functions and most importantly the ring tone. Dom knew getting used to that ring tone could be vital. On an earlier deployment working with an undercover officer, they were sitting around a dinner table in a restaurant with a couple of gangsters. The other undercover officer had put his phone on the table. During the meal, his phone started to ring but the undercover officer ignored it. One of the bemused gangsters asked him why he wasn't answering. The simple answer was that UCO hadn't familiarised himself with that ring tone so didn't recognise it as his.

Chapter 22: The Ice Cream Man

J ust after seven-thirty there was a knock on the door. Bob looked through the hotel room door spyhole and saw Andy's features grotesquely distorted by the fish-eye lens in the spyhole glass. Nevertheless, it was Andy, so Bob let him enter. Andy was dressed in his going out clothes. He was all in white except for the red laces in his white trainers. He was wearing white tracksuit bottoms, and a white T-shirt under a white puffer jacket. Bob asked him, "What have you come dressed as? An ice cream man?"

Cue lots of laughter at Andy's expense, but it didn't bother him. He crossed the room and made a beeline for Dom and greeted him like a long-lost brother. "Dom, you're looking well, mate. I got to say when I heard it was you coming up I was over the moon. You'll run circles round these Geordie muppets."

Andy released Dom from the man-hug then greeted Tracey with a light hug and peck on the cheek. Tracey raised her hand to her cheek when Andy said, "Are you rubbing that off or rubbing it in, darling?"

"Definitely not in. Is that what you're going out in tonight?" Tracey said.

Andy first greeted Bob and Terry with a handshake but with

a wink, he said, "This is the height of Italian fashion in the smoke, believe me. Geordies will all be wearing this in another five years when they catch up."

Tracey had to get in the last word. "I agree with Bob, you look like a fucking ice cream man. You've got to get changed, Andy. Please."

The room settled down and Tracey, Andy and Dom developed their legend story.

Dom was Andy's uncle and had a haulage business in the Manchester area. He was in trouble with the VAT man and had been given a deadline to pay an outstanding VAT bill. He was worried about getting involved and caught, facing jail time. Tracey had heard Andy talking about his Uncle Dom but didn't know him that well. This was only the second time she had met him, the first was at a family party at a golf club somewhere around Manchester that ended up in a family punch-up in the car park. Dom's sister, Anna, was Andy's mum but sadly she died when Andy was a kid, and he was brought up in London by his dad, Jimmy, an alcoholic, and that's what killed him some years ago. Andy was a bit of a Jack the Lad and had his sticky fingers into all sorts of shenanigans.

Andy already had a conversation with Chris about the possibility of someone who might be able to help with nicking the load of booze. That someone would be Uncle Dom, who was in a corner and needed a leg up. Andy would tell Chris about Dom but leave out the bit about him being his uncle. That was best left to Dom to drop it on Chris out of the blue. Everyone was clear on the story, but Dom stressed to Andy that once he was into Chris, Andy was to drop off the radar and leave it to him. Finally, Andy told Dom to ask for him and Tracey at the door to the bar and he would be given VIP access. *Something straight out of Andy's play book*, thought Dom. Bob pointed out that if this lorry load job came off, Tracey's flat would be burnt, of no further use, and she would have to move out. This would have to be coordinated with the arrest phase of the operation to avoid looking suspicious or leaving her out there when everyone was nicked. This was Bob's responsibility and sat squarely in his court.

Once everyone was comfortable with the story, Andy and Tracey left in the hire car and made their way back to the flat. Tracey had a hide in the flat for her and Andy's recording devices which they used on every deployment and phone calls connected to their deployment.

Dom left the hotel an hour later by taxi with his recording device primed and ready to activate before he walked into the pub. He was hoping that an hour would give the love birds a chance to get back to Tracey's flat, pick up their devices and hopefully, Andy would take the opportunity to change before Dom walked into the bar for the family reunion.

The taxi pulled up directly outside the front door of an up-market city centre bar which had the appearance of a club rather than a bar. Two doormen dressed smartly in dark suits, white shirts and bow ties stood either side of the heavy red ropes supported by brass poles. He made his way to the front of the short queue of people and introduced himself to the doorman and mentioned he was a guest of Andy and Tracey. The doorman made a quick check of the list attached to a clipboard and Dom was ushered into the bar and pointed towards the VIP area. The bar was packed, and he had to jostle his way towards another doorman standing at the entrance to the VIP area.

As Dom finally reached the doorman, he heard Tracey call

his name and she told the doorman he was with them. Andy, still in his ice cream man outfit, and Tracey fitted in well with the clientele who enjoyed having room to move around the VIP area, unlike the customers in the main bar. Dom took a seat at the table next to Tracey as Andy offered him a glass of champagne from the half empty bottle in an ice bucket in the centre of their table. Dom could already see where Terry's money was going. Dom had never been a piss-taker around expenses and had pulled up UCOs on operations he was covering for kicking the arse out of the budget. On one job, a female UCO tried to put a jar of expensive face cream through on her expenses, claiming that was the product she used in her real life. Dom politely but firmly suggested she brought her own cream and to re-submit her expenses less the ninety-five-pound jar of face cream.

Dom declined the champagne and asked the waiter for a single Jameson in a tall glass with lots of ice. This was a crafty trick Dom had developed over the years. Getting drunk and ordering round after round of drinks while deployed and recording is asking for trouble. It's not a good tactic to pour drinks down your throat and that of the targets' and then produce the tape in court at a later day. Dom preferred to nurse the drink, letting the ice melt to maintain the level of liquid in the glass to last him for prolonged periods.

Andy told Dom that Chris had been in the bar when he and Tracey arrived. They'd had a brief chat with him before he slipped out for something he had to deal with, but he was coming back. "All I've said, mate, is that you were up here for a few days, and he might want to have a chat with you about the forty-footer and you've got a cash flow problem with the VAT man. I've said nothing more," Andy said.

"Okay, buddy, that's good, just drop me the nod when he comes back in. It's a bit full and noisy in here," Dom said whilst thinking about the quality of the recording, as he didn't want to lose any of the evidential recorded conversation owing to background noise. He'd been faced with this situation before and knew how he was going to deal with it.

Occasionally, some men and women came across to say hello to Andy and Tracey. Tracey seemed to be popular with the other bar goers and had a few dances with the other girls. Andy was his usual flash self, talking loudly in his cockney accent. His all-white outfit looked even more ridiculous under the neon lighting. Some of the local lads were taking the piss out of Andy and the way he spoke but he didn't seem to mind. *Maybe he thought it was a form of acceptance by the locals,* Dom thought. Still nursing his Jameson on ice, Dom felt a tap on his foot. It was Andy. He nodded towards the entrance and mouthed, "Chris."

Chapter 23: The VIP Area

Dom saw a man in his thirties facing the doorman who was performing access control to the VIP area. Both men were standing close to each other, exchanging something hand to hand. Dom had seen small drug deals go down many times before and this fitted the bill. Following this transaction, Chris made his way to the bar and had a quick chat with a couple. He then walked towards the gents' toilet, followed by the male half of the couple he had just been talking to. Both men disappeared into the loo and reappeared a couple of minutes later and went their own ways.

After ten minutes, Dom instructed Andy to call Chris over. Andy got to his feet and called out, "Chris, Chris, over here, mate." Chris came across and Andy did the intros. "Dom, meet Chris, Chris meet Dom." That was it. Dom was in, and Chris was at the start of a journey that would end in jail time. Andy and Tracey left, leaving Dom and Chris sharing the table.

Dom wasn't going to make it easy for Chris or too difficult. He was going to play it just right. He decided on a bit of small talk without giving anything up. Chris made it easy for Dom by mentioning Manchester and connecting it to football, a subject that Dom was able to talk about all day. He'd been a Manchester United supporter all his life and was comfortable exchanging 'footy talk' with supporters of other clubs. Chris was a big fan of the Toon, Newcastle United, and both men traded verbal blows with each other over their respective teams. In a subtle way, Dom mentioned his haulage business but didn't linger on the subject. But he did notice Chris had picked up on it as he was trying to bring the conversation back round to it.

Chris looked round the room and caught the eye of one of the waiters. "Fancy a drink, Dom?"

Dom looked at his glass which he had been nursing now for over an hour. "Yeah, thanks. I'll have a Jameson in a tall glass with lots of ice please, mate." He handed his glass to the waiter.

Chris turned to the waiter. "I'll have my usual, in fact make it a double, Chaz."

As soon as the drinks arrived Chris continued his probing conversation about haulage. "Andy tells me you have haulage contracts up this neck of the woods, Dom, is that what brings you up here today?"

Dom explained there were so many rules and regulations and paperwork in the transport industry today that it was a minefield. Chris's eyes glazed over. It seemed like he was getting tired of the shadow boxing and moved the conversation on. "How long have you known Andy?" Chris asked.

"All his life, I'm his uncle."

Chris smiled. "The little cockney knob never mentioned that. He said he knew someone in the haulage game that might be able to help me and my mate out. A case of you scratch my back and I'll scratch yours."

"That's the way the lad has been brought up. He has his little hands in all sorts of pies and plays his cards close to his chest. Not a bad thing sometimes. His dad was a wrong 'un, drank himself into an early grave. Look at the flash Harry," Dom nodded in Andy's direction, "on the pop with his champagne. I can see him ending up like his dad. Not my business, he's big enough to look after himself."

Chris drew closer. "Listen, Dom, I know you've got a bit of a cashflow situation right now. What about you and my mate having a sit down round the table to see how we can help each other? Just a chat for now, no promises. What do you say?"

"I'm open to a chat with your mate, who is he?"

"Ian, he's like my boss. I do the odd job for him now and then. He's a top bloke, everyone loves him. He'll like you even if you're a Manc."

"That's all well and good, I know the value of a load and I know what I need to clean my slate with the VAT man. I also know what will happen to me if this goes wrong. I'd be up shit creek without a paddle. I've never done anything like this before and the thought of going to jail outweighs the VAT man chasing me."

Chris said, "Dom, let me tell you, we've done this before. We got everything covered. Have a sit down with Ian and me and we'll talk you through it and we can sort out the figures."

Dom asked, "Why do you need me if you've done this before? Why not use the same guy again?"

"Because using the same fella again will bring the pains on him from the law. To lose one load is bad luck, to lose a second is fucking suspicious. So, you do one job with us, have your pay day and you never hear or see us again. That's us looking out for you, Dom."

Dom hesitated, giving Chris the impression he was unsure and anxious about any criminal enterprise with Chris and his boss Ian. He asked Chris for his phone number. Chris called over to Chaz, the waiter, and used his notepad to scribble down his number. Dom told him he didn't care to talk too much in the bar in case people overheard them and he wanted to think things over. Chris agreed, and handed the scrap of paper to Dom. "I'll call you tomorrow," Dom said as he placed the paper into his pocket. Dom was playing out the game plan as agreed at the briefing prior to his deployment. Once Chris had given over his number, he returned to the bar and picked up on his other business, leaving Dom at the table.

After sitting alone for a few minutes mulling over his next move, Tracey and Andy returned and finished off the bottle of bubbles. Dom asked Andy to call him a cab to pick him up in ten minutes outside to take him back to his hotel. He finished his drink and said good night to the love birds as Andy was ordering a second bottle, paying in cash with a ten-pound tip to Chaz, the waiter. As he was leaving the VIP lounge, Chris looked across at Dom and held his hand to his ear mimicking a phone call. Dom looked back, smiled and nodded then discreetly waved at Chris. By the time Dom had pushed his way from the bar onto the pavement, the taxi had arrived. The driver lowered the window and asked Dom if he was for the Double Tree Hotel. Once inside the cab, Dom deactivated the device. He took his phone from his pocket and texted Bob to say he was on his way back.

Chapter 24: Ian Maloney

On entering the hotel room, Bob and Terry were sharing a bottle of white wine. A third person was also present, so Dom was introduced to Dave, a member of the operational team. Dave's job was to make notes from Dom's debrief and accept his exhibits.

"Fancy a glass, mate?" Bob asked as he raised the half full bottle.

"No, but thanks, mate," Dom said pulling his bottle of Jameson out of his suitcase. Dom gave a brief account of his visit to the bar and his conversation with Chris. When Dom mentioned Ian's name, Bob and Terry looked at each other and smiled. "Something I said?" asked Dom.

Terry raised his wine glass as if he was toasting Dom and said, "Ian. That could be, probably definitely might be, Ian Maloney, core nominal of this parish and the main target of the operation. That little cockney has only done what we're paying him to do. It isn't cocaine but I'll take it."

Dom completed his notes. Before placing the scrap of paper with Chris's phone number into an exhibit bag, Dom entered the number into the contacts on his burner phone. He also put his recording into an exhibit bag and handed both over to Dave. Terry signed off Dom's notes. Once the business of the day had been completed, the team moved on how to take the next step forward. Several options were discussed, but it was agreed that Dom would call Chris and arrange a meeting with him and Ian towards the end of the following week. This delay would give the team some time to do additional authorities and arrange a surveillance team to evidence the meeting. Owing to Dom's notional business commitments, he would ask them to travel to Hartshead Moor Service Station on the M62 motorway. Dom still planned to sound a bit flaky about getting involved in the theft but was tempted by the possibility of a good payday. The delay would also allow Bob to contact the Manchester undercover unit to secure the services of a UCO known as Titch to be deployed on this job. Dom and Titch had worked together before and had a tried and tested backstory between them that could withstand a degree of scrutiny. They were also confident in each other's abilities.

Another debrief had been arranged for Tracey and Andy at ten o'clock the following morning. Dom was also needed at that debrief. It was agreed that the introduction of Titch into the plan and the meeting at Hartshead Moor was not to be disclosed. There was good reason for this. It's far better for the UCOs to discover some details first revealed by the opposition, OCG members. In that way, the UCOs can react naturally, having heard the news for the first time. Dom had been to debriefs on previous deployments where he had walked in with what he believed to be a golden nugget of new intelligence, only to find out it was already known to the operation team. But his reaction on first hearing the intelligence on the plot was totally natural.

Everything agreed, the three operational team members departed, and Dom refreshed his Jameson and settled down on the bed to watch TV and relax.

At ten o'clock the following morning the three operational team members and the three undercover officers gathered in Dom's hotel room. Andy informed the group that Chris had approached him after Dom had left and nutted into him about Dom. In Andy's lingo that meant he was questioned about Dom. Nothing too deep. Andy also reported the usual drug dealing by the usual suspects and some chat about ambushing away fans at the next home game against Chelsea. Tracey confirmed Andy's account but added the bit about her identifying two girls scoring charlie, cocaine, in the girls' loo from a female dealer they already knew about.

Once all exhibits and PNBs had been completed, Bob, using the excuse that the account holder wanted to complete the finances for signing off, asked Andy to complete his expenses before leaving. Andy moved over to a small round table and pulled a bundle of receipts from his rucksack. Bob handed him a couple of blank sheets of A4 expenses forms and an envelope. About half an hour later, Andy had finished his chore so handed the envelope, now bulging with forms and receipts, to Bob. Before Tracey and Andy left, they gave Dom a hug and wished him well, knowing that if everything went well they wouldn't be seeing Dom again on this operation. Once Andy and Tracey had left, Bob pulled the A4 expenses sheet from the envelope and glanced briefly at the bottom line before handing it to Terry, the DI.

"Bloody hell, Bob! That's the equivalent to a small country's GDP. You will have to have a word with him, mate. I can't keep justifying these numbers. I know we're moving forward but at what price?" Terry said.

Bob agreed and looked across at Dom with a 'told you so'

look.

Dom wanted to call Chris before he set off south and waited until just after midday before doing so. He prepared his recording device and using the burner phone he brought up Chris's number. He asked Dave to take the house phone off the hook and everyone to switch their phones off or to silent. Chris's phone rang three or four times before he answered it.

"Hello." *A man of few words*, thought Dom.

Chapter 25: Text Message

"Hi, is that Chris? It's Dom here."

"Yeah, sorry Dom, I didn't recognise the number. Are you all right?"

Dom explained he had slept on their conversation and wanted to have a chat with Ian at the end of the following week. He told Chris that he was returning south after the call and wondered if Ian would do him a favour and meet up on the M62 at Hartshead Moor service station. Dom went on to tell Chris he was flat out with work and couldn't afford to miss out on a load by meeting now. "You'd be doing me a big favour," Dom added.

Chris said, "Right, I don't think it would be a problem. What day is good for you?"

"I can do Thursday or Friday after two on either day, Chris. Ask your mate and get back to me by phone or text me. I appreciate it. I know it's a bit of a hike for you, but I can't be away from the business for too long. Every penny counts. Cheers, mate."

Chris confirmed he would get hold of Ian and see what he said but didn't think it would be a deal breaker, and he would back to Dom as soon as he knew. Both men said their farewells and ended the call. Dom ensured the call had completely shut off. He made a quick time check on the recording and switched the device off. After completing the paperwork, he packed his bag, not forgetting his beloved Jameson, and said goodbye to the others. Bob planned to keep the room on for Andy and Tracey's debrief before Andy flew back to London the following day.

Dom returned to his off-site location on Monday morning and was a little concerned and disappointed that Chris had not contacted him. He called Bob and asked if Tracey or Andy had picked up on any dramas from Chris in the bar after the last phone call between Dom and Chris. Reassuringly, Bob told Dom that they had been in the bar that night and didn't see Chris but didn't sense any bad vibes. Somewhat relieved, but still disappointed, Dom got on with sorting out his diary for the week, writing 'Lorry Job' across the pages of Thursday and Friday. Just before lunch, his burner phone vibrated on his desk. It was a text message from Chris.

Thursday at 2 bell me

Dom was straight on the phone to Bob to bring him up to speed. He wasn't going to call Chris right away. He wanted to drive to the local industrial estate where he could walk round the various roads and factory and storage units, picking up the sounds of vehicles manoeuvring and other voices in the background as he spoke to Chris on the phone. Dom knew little touches like that painted a picture for a target and let them walk into it. Good tradecraft, as he would say.

About two hours later, Dom was parked up on a busy industrial estate a few miles from his off-site office. This was an ideal location, with lorries moving around and the sound of the reversing back-up beeper going off. The gang of workers around the burger van were always a good source of background noise. Dom wanted Chris to hear these noises as part of the illusion. Dom had taken a recording device from the safe prior to leaving his office. This one was slightly different to the usual device. He could attach the device to the phone and record both sides of the conversation whilst holding the phone to his ear as he walked about. To the uneducated eye, Dom was having a conversation on his phone in the same way as any other guy.

Dom waited until three lorries pulled up outside the gates to a large storage unit. He knew the lorries would need to reverse with the unmistakable sound of the beeper and the sound of the engine revving. Whilst he was sorting out his device and phone, one of the lorries began to manoeuvre. The sounds were music to Dom's ears. Perfect. He activated the recording device and made an introduction, referring to the text he had received from Chris earlier that day. Dom got out of his car and walked over to the manoeuvring lorry. As he did so, he rang Chris's number. The phone was answered after one ring.

Dom could hardly hear Chris's voice over the sound of the reversing lorry. "Hello, Dom."

"Hi, Chris, thanks for the text, mate..." Before Dom could say anything more, Chris interrupted.

"Dom, I can't hear a fucking word. All I can hear is a beep beep beep and a fucking engine revving."

"Hang on, Chris, I can't hear a word, let me move away, mate." Dom smiled as he walked back towards his car.

Once he was able to talk and hear what was being said, Dom stopped but the sounds of the industrial estate could still be heard in the background. Chris confirmed the location and time of their meeting with Ian on the westbound carriageway of the M62 at Hartshead Moor Services. Dom asked Chris to pass on his thanks to Ian for travelling down and ended the call.

Back in his car, Dom made sure the phone had shut down. He made a time check on the recording and deactivated the device. He then called Bob and gave him the details of the meeting. Dom was aware of the hive of activity his call would generate for the operational team, but he had bought them three days to get it all done.

Later that day, Bob rang Dom to confirm he had booked a conference room in the Village Hotel, Hyde as a briefing location. He had selected this hotel as it had easy access to the motorway system around Manchester and would give Dom ample opportunity to clean himself, shake off any surveillance when he left the service station, and he would be travelling in a natural direction towards Manchester. Terry was busy getting all his ducks in a line sorting out a surveillance team, photographer, and a reconnaissance of the service station. He also had a trusted contact at the Scottish and Newcastle brewery: a retired police officer who held a senior position within their security department and had helped Terry on previous jobs. However, the brewery stipulated the Northumberland Police insured the load to the value for £311,040, representing the retail value of the load including VAT. Terry had never lost a load yet and he wasn't about to start with this one.

Later that afternoon, Titch called Dom using his legend phone to tell him that he had been given the green light to work with him and if possible, to avoid Wednesdays for any deployments as he took his daughter to drum lessons after school, and he would hate letting her down.

Dom knew Titch well enough to go in for a bit of leg-pulling.

"Good to hear from you, mate, and I'm glad it's you. Don't worry, I'll explain to the gangsters that Wednesdays are out because Titch is playing drums. Speak soon, mate. Bye."

Thursday morning arrived and Dom was driving towards the hotel on the outskirts of east Manchester. Hyde is famous or infamous for several reasons. The boxer, Ricky Hatton, is a great guy but a big Manchester City fan which put him on the blue side of Manchester, whereas Dom was a red. Doctor Harold Shipman, possibly the biggest mass murderer in history, and in the sixties, those murdering shit bags Brady and Hindley. He hoped the last three were still burning in hell. Dom grew up around Manchester where those defenceless children were snatched by those evil bastards. His emotions surrounding that period of his life had always been just below the surface. This was to be the first of two sad journeys into Dom's memories on that day. The second was to come later at the motorway.

Dom pulled into the car park of the Village hotel and found a parking space close to the entrance. He noticed Bob's car and dropped him a text to let him know he was in the car park. Shortly after, Bob tapped on the side window of his car. Dom, getting out of his car, greeted Bob with a handshake. Bob, looking like he'd been up all night, took Dom's hand. "We've got to stop meeting like this, mate, people are starting to talk," Dom said.

They made their way into the meeting room on the ground floor of the hotel where Terry and Dave were both busy on their phones in opposite corners to avoid disturbing each other. Bob made Dom a cup of tea. Handing it to Dom, they waited for the other two to end their calls.

"Morning, Dom," Dave said as he refilled his now lukewarm coffee. "The gear you've got on now, mate, is that exactly what you will be wearing on the plot today?"

"Yeah, what's wrong with it?"

"Nothing, you know what's coming next," Dave continued. "The surveillance team want to know. The boss decided to let the targets run free [no surveillance] from Newcastle. Why risk the chance of a compromise? Our surveillance team is waiting in their cars outside in the car park. So, before you get too comfortable, come and have a quick trot outside, so they know who they're looking at on the plot."

This was a common practice for a surveillance team. Another method, which Dom didn't like, was taking a photo of the UCO and passing it round in their briefing. Another option was for the UCO to put in a guest appearance at the surveillance team briefing. This method made Dom feel a bit like a male model on the catwalk. He felt like doing one of those sultry poses, thrusting his hips out and pouting his lips as the team took in his appearance.

Dave and Dom walked to the car park and as they did so, Dave called the surveillance team commander to inform him they were on their way. They stopped on the corner of the car park just as the exiting traffic slowed down to join the main road. In less than a minute, a convoy of five cars, a motorcycle and a van departed, heading towards the motorway. The convoy's eyes were on Dom. Then Dom and Dave returned to their tea and coffee.

Back in the room, Terry, Bob and Dave formally debriefed and took Dom's exhibits from his call with Chris. This was followed by a briefing for the next stage. At the end of the meeting Terry handed Dom a yellow Post-it® note. "You want to inwardly digest the figures on that note, Dom, it might come in handy later." Dom looked at the information written on the note and put it in his jacket pocket, then made his way back to the car park.

Chapter 26: Hartshead Moor

Hartshead Moor is the highest motorway service station in the United Kingdom and has a footbridge enabling people to cross from one side to the other safely, high above the fast-moving traffic. It is situated almost equal distance between junctions 25 and 26 of the motorway. Dom decided to give himself enough time to go beyond the service area and do a U-turn at junction 26, so that he was on the westbound carriageway ready for his journey back to Manchester.

Having completed his U-turn at junction 26, Dom indicated left as he passed the countdown markers for the service station. He was twenty minutes early for a personal reason, and not the operational one of arriving before Ian and Chris, allowing him the opportunity to pick the table and his seat to give the surveillance team the best view of the subjects.

He parked in a marked bay close to a memorial erected in the memory of those murdered by the IRA on 4 February 1974. A bomb had been planted on a civilian operated coach returning soldiers and families from Manchester to Catterick Garrison in North Yorkshire. The bomb exploded, killing twelve people. Two of them were children, Robert aged two, and his brother Lee who was five. Their parents, Corporal Clifford and his wife, Linda, were also killed. The bombing had taken place five months into Dom's military career. Dom spent a few minutes remembering the victims and other mates he'd lost during his time serving his country. As he turned away, he quietly muttered, "God bless you. May you all rest in peace."

Game head back on, Dom popped back into his car and made the usual introduction into the recording device and refreshed his memory with the information on the yellow note and put it back in his pocket. Knowing that the surveillance team would now have eyes on him, Dom walked into the building housing various food and drink outlets. At a self-service counter, Dom scanned the area as he was making his tea. The tea bag came in one of those small individual stainless-steel teapots that held just enough for one cuppa. There was no sign of Chris and a table for four had just become available by the window overlooking the carriageway. Dom made a beeline to the empty table and sat sideways next to the floor to ceiling glass window and waited.

He didn't have to wait long when he saw Chris and another guy walk into the seating area carrying Starbucks takeaway paper cups. Dom waited until they got closer, then waved to catch Chris's attention. Chris acknowledged Dom and headed his way.

"Hi, Dom, how you are doing? This is my mate, Ian, who I told you about."

"Hello, Ian, good of you to travel down here. It's just that..."

Before Dom could finish, Ian stopped him. "Listen, man, it's no problem. I'm in and out of Newcastle all the time, this run out here today is nothing. Don't worry about it. Drink your tea before it goes cold."

"I don't think it was that hot to start with," Dom said.

As Dom poured the tea from the steel pot into the cup, he tipped the pot just too far. The lid on the teapot wasn't tight shut and the tea slopped out. Some of it found its target, the cup, but a good amount splashed onto the table. Dom, not one to miss an opportunity said, "Oh God, for fuck's sake. Look, I'm sorry, lads. I'm all over the place with my nerves. What with the VAT man and everything else."

Chris went to get some napkins to soak up the tea while Ian set about reassuring Dom that everything would be sweet. Chris returned and did a good job cleaning up the tea and sat back down. Then the two men set about sounding out Dom, firing off questions about his firm, contracts and how much money was he looking for. Dom had prepared himself well for this part of the meeting. He was able to talk in depth about his haulage business. He didn't portray his business as a massive operation, more of a family established company that had been passed down from his dad. He had gathered contract knowledge over the years and Terry's mate at Scottish and Newcastle had filled him in on the procedures on site, particularly about tracking devices secreted in their loads. Dom told them that the runs were unpredictable and operated on a supply and demand basis. He told them how it usually worked: the customer placed an order with Scottish and Newcastle and they contacted their contractors. Whoever picked up the phone first and was available got the run. Drivers never knew if the load was being tracked.

Ian told Dom not to worry about trackers as he had an inside man who would make sure there wouldn't be a tracker on his load. Chris asked about trackers on Dom's tractor units.

"No, no need. I can track my lorries on an app on my mobile, but I hardly ever use it. I can just phone my driver and ask him.

Old fashioned but effective."

Ian, sounding a bit uncomfortable, asked, "How much are you looking for, Dom?"

Dom reached into his pocket and produced the yellow Post-it® note. Placing it on the table, Ian and Chris saw what was written on it. Dom slowly traced his forefinger over a line at a time as he read out the numbers.

"Right. We pull a forty-foot trailer holding thirty-six pallets, thirty-six cases on a pallet, a case contains twelve bottles. That adds up to fifteen thousand, five hundred and fifty-two bottles. Retail value £311,040. I appreciate that's supermarket retail and knock off will be less and I'm working on fifty percent less, so let's say that load is going to be in the ballpark area of £155,500."

Still mesmerised by the numbers, Ian said, without raising his head, "You've done your homework, Dom, and I can't argue with the figures or what you're saying." Then he looked at Dom and continued, "How much do you need to pay off the VAT man?"

Dom paused for a second. "Thirty grand and some change. But I want a few quid for me out of this and I'll have to bung the driver something."

Eyes locked on Dom, Ian said, "What's your corner then, Dom? Let's not piss about, give me a number."

Picking up the note, Dom studied the numbers as he relaxed back into his chair. "I'll have the fifty-five grand and take care of the driver out of my corner."

Ian and Chris looked at each other before Ian said, "That's more than we were thinking of, mate. I got the guy on the inside to pay and he's taking a fucking big risk. Then, I've got a distribution operation to set up and pay for, and Chris is on a pay day. We're going to have to do something with the figures, mate."

Reluctant to walk away, Dom knew he had to make this look and sound right. He had to make the right noises over the money.

"Like your fella on the inside, I'm taking a hell of a risk on this, and I think it's worth good money."

"Why don't you drive the lorry and save yourself some dosh?" Chris said.

"You're joking. The only time I drive a wagon now is if there is no one else. If I was suddenly out on the road and I lose the load it's going to look wrong, and the cops will be all over me. No, I've got a driver. Ian, you're getting two-thirds and I'm getting a third. We both have overheads."

Ian smiled at Dom. "You can tell you've been in business all your life, Dom. You make good sense, and you know your way round the numbers. Okay, fifty-five grand, but I can't pay until after the job, mate. I don't have that sort of cash to hand."

"Without sounding rude or causing any offence, that is a lot of trust to place in two guys I've only just met. As you say, I'm a businessman and I would be looking at some assurance or insurance that everything will turn out right at the end. No offence, lads, but I'm sure you would be the same if the shoe was on the other foot."

Ian still smiling said, "Dom, you're dead right. I would have thought you'd be mad not to have something up front. I'll put ten grand in your pocket to go with your little yellow note at our next meeting if we shake hands on the deal here and now. Okay?"

Reaching across the table Dom offered his hand and said, "You couldn't make it thirty grand up front, could you?"

Ian saw the twinkle in his eyes. "Now you are taking the piss. Ten grand and the rest when I sell the booty within two weeks. I've already got sixty to seventy percent of the load placed with my regulars. Now let's talk about the lad that's going to drive the lorry."

"Yeah, Titch, he's a top lad with a clean record, only because he's never been caught. He knows how to keep his mouth shut and stay off the radar," Dom said.

"He's never done anything like this before?" Ian asked but before Dom could answer, Ian continued, "Listen, Dom, I'll be up front with you. When this goes down your lad is going to spend an uncomfortable few days getting grilled by the cops. It won't be the local uniforms or CID. They'll bring in the big boys from the crime squad. They won't fuck about."

That made Dom smile inside, knowing Ian was talking to a National Crime Squad undercover officer. He wanted to say, *They are already here, you muppet.*

Instead, Dom said, "I'll have to give you a call once I've sat down and had a chat with him. I'll give you a shout in the next few days. I assume I'll get my insurance payment at our next meeting?"

"Yeah, sure," replied Ian.

After some chat about football and their clubs' last few games, all three walked to the car park. To Dom's surprise, he saw Chris and Ian had parked almost next to Dom's Mercedes. It turned out Ian had told Chris that they should have parked on the other side and used the footbridge as now they had to drive in the opposite direction to spin round. Dom thought, *That explains why they are parked on this side of the motorway.*

Ian then mentioned the memorial, but Dom didn't respond because he didn't want to engage in unnecessary conversation.

Farewells and a final handshake over, the three men drove off in a convoy. But first, Dom switched off the recording device before he pulled away in pole position. Indicating right to join the motorway, Dom saw Chris and Ian directly behind him followed by several nondescript vehicles mixed in with a lorry. As Dom passed the exit to junction twenty-five, he looked in his mirror and saw Chris exit and flash his headlights. Dom switched on his four-way flashers for two or three flashes and made his way to the Village hotel. The surveillance team let Chris and Ian run free. There was no need to take any risks if Chris and Ian were looking for a surveillance team after having a dirty meeting.

Chapter 27: Steak and Kidney Pudding

A rriving at the Hyde meeting room, Dom found Terry, Dave and Bob sitting around the table, finishing off a tray of sandwiches. Dom looked at what was left and chose to eat later after the debrief. He complimented Terry on the yellow Post-it® and produced it as an exhibit together with his recording. Terry took a call from the surveillance commander, telling him that the meeting was evidenced by video and still photography together with individual officers' written observations. The subject of the surveillance was confirmed as Ian Maloney.

After the debrief, Dom set off and stopped at the first English fish and chip shop he found. He bought his favourite Hollands of Baxenden steak and kidney pudding with chips and mushy peas in a tray with gravy. *You can take the boy out of Manchester, but you can't take Manchester out of the boy*, he thought, sitting in his car outside the chippy as he polished off what he regarded as a three-star Michelin meal, washed down with his favourite childhood treat, a can of fizzy dandelion and burdock. With plenty of childhood memories for company, he drove home.

That weekend Dom spent time with his family doing dad and husband things. His children grew up in a very middle-class environment. They lived in a five-bedroom detached house in a village in middle England. They went to a combined village school that had fifty pupils at most. They had gone on an aeroplane before they travelled on a bus or train. They didn't know what it was like to go without or get a whack from Dad, unlike their father's childhood. Dom had two daughters from his first marriage, Lesley and Jayne, who were great role models to their younger siblings. Dom had first married whilst serving in the Army. That marriage ended in divorce before Dom joined the police force in his thirties. Unlike Judy, his first wife never experienced the loneliness of the wife of an undercover cop. Despite the nature of his job, Dom's family were a close supportive group who looked out for each other. None of his children were spoilt, and they understood the concept of respect and the value of hard work.

To emphasise these values, Dom, with his kids in the car, would sometimes detour into the council estates like the one he grew up in Manchester. He would drive around the streets where the gardens were littered with old sofas, stained mattresses, black plastic rubbish sacks, other detritus too disgusting to mention, and cars with no wheels jacked up on bricks. There were groups of youths smoking and hanging round the shop, racing along the footpaths on probably stolen bikes. Dom would say, "If you don't work hard at school and you get involved in drugs and crime, this is where you will live, and these people will be your friends." Harsh but true, and Dom knew he delivered this message with honesty and conviction because that was the environment he had grown up in.

It must have hit home because his daughter, Rochelle, who had her own pet name, BB, short for Baby Breath from her breathing pattern as a toddler, had been talking to her friends about her tour of the estate. As a result, one night in the local village pub some of Dom's friends and neighbours asked him to take their kids on the 'terror trip' as they called it.

It was good for Dom to relax over the weekend, having a few beers with his mates and taking his boy Alexander to football on Sunday morning. Alexander also had a pet name, H, short for head because when he was born, he had an oversized head, well out of proportion with his body. His children felt special with their pet names. Their friends went by conventional shortened versions of their Christian names or pet names their parents used, but BB and H had letters from the alphabet. This time with his family was invaluable as it also allowed him to recharge his batteries for the following week and whatever might come his way.

Monday morning arrived, and Dom decided to work from the dining room at home, completing reports, expenses and a set of transcripts from a previous deployment which was going to Crown Court in the next few months. Dom didn't need to ask his boss, Kath, if he could work from home. She had been his boss for some time and knew he would be putting a shift in and not sitting around watching TV with his feet up. Dom's dining room was his remote office and when Dad went in there with a hand full of phones, the kids knew he wasn't available for dad stuff. There were two BT landline phones in the dining room. One was an extension of the house phone; the other was on a Manchester code 0161. Using the Manchester number, he called Titch's covert number.

"Hi, Titch, mate, has Bob been in touch with you yet?"

"Yeah, I've given him a couple of days for this week but not Wednesday. Thursday or Friday works for me. Or Saturday morning as a last resort, I've got to be away by two at the latest for my mum's birthday."

"Yeah, okay, I'm flexible on any of those. I'll give Bob a bell. Speak to you later, mate."

Before Dom hung up, Titch shouted, "Before you go, you've come up on a Manchester number, are you around here?"

"No, mate, I'm at home."

"Shame, I've got tickets to the match tonight we could have had a night out watching a top team, a few beers and a curry."

"I'd rather stick a red-hot poker in my eye than watch City, thanks. Speak later," Dom said chuckling as he replaced the handset.

Dom put the headphones on and got on with his transcripts. He knew that one hour of conversation took around eight hours to transcribe. On some occasions, the operational team would have an audio typist produce a transcript but there would be so many parts marked as 'Inaudible' that the undercover officer would spend hours deciphering the speech on the tape. He hated doing transcripts, but it came with the job. After a couple of hours of stop, rewind, play, stop, rewind, and play again, he was relieved to see his covert phone dance across the dining table on vibrate. Thank God.

"Hi Bob, what's the news?"

Bob told Dom that everything was set at his end for Saturday morning and if Dom could convince Maloney to travel to the same services that would be great for Titch, but he wouldn't commit hari-kari if the plans had to change. Dom knew Titch's plans for Saturday, and they would use his mum's birthday to their advantage.

"Okay, I'll bell Chris this evening and run it by him. It gives them almost a week to sort it out. I'll push for Saturday morning around ten or eleven at Hartshead Moor, mate. Bye."

Later that day Dom stood at the school gates doing the dad thing, picking up H. Dom looked round the other parents waiting with him, recognised every one of them and knew some as good friends. It was a small community, and everyone knew everyone and their business, but they didn't know Dom's business. Part of him wanted to join their chit chat about what they had been doing over the last few days. Sometimes, he wanted to share the excitement of doing deals for over a quarter of a million pounds of stolen property or drug deals for kilos of cocaine or heroin. But he couldn't. The other parents just looked on him as a policeman who worked on CID somewhere. Dom felt like screaming, "No, I do this..."

Back home after tea and kicking a football around the back garden with H, Dom thought of putting a call into Chris and how he was going to approach him, but his son wrapped himself around Dom's leg to stop him getting to the ball and this brought his attention back to H and the game. BB then came out and told them that Mum had put dinner on the table. After dinner, it was back to his alternative world.

After dinner, Dom went into the dining room with a hand full of phones and a recording device. H and BB knew not to disturb him and to keep the noise down. Dom switched on the TV but adjusted the volume, so it was just loud enough to be heard in the background when he made his call to Chris. Background noise is natural and paints the desired picture. The recording device was ready to go and the TV playing low in the background when Dom called Chris's number.

Chapter 28: Kick Around

"All right Dom, what's happening?"

"Good thanks, Chris. I've just been having a kick around with my little fella in the garden and he whacked me in the shin. I think he might have broken my leg."

"I know what you mean, man, my lad's a lunatic with a football, you just can't get it off him. He'll play for the Toon one day."

"I hope he does, Chris, that would be brilliant," Dom said but thought, *You might have to watch it on TV from your cell on Match of the Day.*

"How we doing with your lad Titch, any news?"

Dom explained that Titch would only be available at a weekend because he was 'nights out' [away from home overnight on a driving job] during the week Monday to Friday. He knew he had to get Chris to agree to two things: Firstly, the time and day, and secondly the location. He decided to get Chris to agree to point one first.

"Is a Saturday morning good for you and Ian, mate?"

"No, man, we work twenty-four seven, seven days a week, fifty-two weeks a year with no time off for Christmas."

Both laughed and Dom added, "Yeah, I know what you mean. Money is money when and wherever you can find it."

Day and time sorted, on to the next point. Dom thought, *Let's cut straight to the chase and not fuck about.* "That's great, what about the same place we meet before?" Dom said.

"Yeah, why not, it's only down the road for us."

"Well, that's a date. Shall we say around nine o'clock?"

"I'll speak with Ian, but I don't think he'll have an issue. I'll get back to you one way or the other, mate."

Before the call ended, Dom said, "Take some advice, Chris, go to the next junction past the services and do a U-ey, then you're on the right side of the motorway to go home and you can use the foot bridge. It will keep Ian off your case."

"Yeah, we had that conversation as we followed you up the road the other day. But thanks for thinking of me."

After he had switched everything off and completed his PNB, Dom called Bob and debriefed him with the latest developments. Bob said that he would book a hotel room for Friday and Saturday night at the Village Hotel if Dom wanted to travel up on Friday and avoid an early start on Saturday morning. The room would be available to him if he wanted to stay over on Saturday night. Bob then called Titch to give him the maximum time to sort his life out for the meeting. Dom packed all his tricky stuff, the recordings, PNB, and recording device into his holdall together with the operational paperwork he'd been working on that day. He took the holdall upstairs and secured it in the hide in his bedroom. Dom always thought if someone broke in during the night, apart from fighting a burglar, the tricky stuff was safe, secure and undetectable.

Skipping downstairs, he walked into the lounge to join his family watching the telly. "What's on?" he asked as he slipped effortlessly from one role to another. He was now the regular family man.

Dom accepted Bob's offer of avoiding an early morning start on Saturday and drove back to Manchester on Friday afternoon, but not before reassuring H he would be back for football on Sunday morning. Prior to checking into the Village Hotel, Dom headed for his three-star Michelin chippy and had his go-to choice from the menu. Checking into the hotel, he could hear and see the hard core of a wedding party in the bar and decided it was a night in front of the TV and his mate Jameson with a bucket of ice, and of course the 'Do Not Disturb' sign hanging on the door handle.

The following morning, he left the sign on the door and made his way to the conference room where Bob was waiting with Titch and Terry. They had already completed the paperwork with Titch and were ready to commence the briefing covering that day's activities. Titch and Dom had worked together on lorry jobs before, so they had a solid back story already in place. They didn't need to take themselves off for a walk around the car park scripting a history. It wasn't long before they set off for the meeting with Ian and Chris.

Before switching on their recording devices and getting out of Dom's Mercedes at the Service Station, Titch reached across and grabbed Dom's arm with a vice like grip. "Who the fuck are you and why are we here?"

Dom looked at Titch and almost whispered, "You're Thelma and I'm Louise and we are about to fuck Chris and Ian." They smiled.

Titch got out and switched on his device and made his

introduction. Dom waited for Titch to shut the car door and he made his introduction. These guys were experienced elite UCOs and knew how important it was not to make an introduction standing by another UCO who has a tape running. This was in case there was ever a successful public interest immunity, PII, application removing one of the UCOs from material disclosed to the defence legal team. Introductions finished, Titch and Dom walked into the services and headed for the counter. They were in good time and there was no sign of Chris and Ian.

Now the devices were running, Dom and Titch didn't speak unless it was necessary. Both men sat in silence until Dom whispered, "Chris and Ian have just walked in and waved in my direction."

Chapter 29: Read the Supplement

Titch nodded in acknowledgement. Chris and Ian were holding their usual Starbucks coffee and walked over to take up the two available seats at the table occupied by Dom and Titch. This was by design. Dom and Titch had purposely left those two seats, giving Chris and Ian a full view of the café. More to the point, the surveillance team using video could eyeball them, capturing a full face-on view of them. After introductions and lots of hand shaking, Ian got down to business. He passed Dom a copy of the *Newcastle Chronicle* across the table.

"I think you'll enjoy reading the supplement, mate," Ian said.

Dom picked up the newspaper and saw the supplement contained a brown envelope.

"Well, you don't hang around, Ian. I'm guessing there are ten thousand reasons to read the supplement," Dom said.

Ian and Chris got down to business and discussed with Dom and Titch how the runs for Scottish and Newcastle worked. Dom explained that Titch hit the road sometimes on a Sunday evening from the docks or on a Monday morning. He tipped [unloaded his cargo] and then drove to pick up another load and then tipped that. He would do that all week, loading then tipping the loads.

Titch chipped in, "He runs me ragged all week, load, tip, load, tip, load, tip, load... all fucking week. But I love it."

Ian asked, "What about the booze runs? Tell me about them."

Titch told Ian he only knew it was a booze run when Dom called him. Dom added he got a call and if he could do it, he'd have a few days' notice and would see which of his drivers was best placed to do the run.

"So, we have to be able to go with a couple of days' notice, Dom?" asked Ian.

"Yeah, that's how it works, mate," Dom said.

Ian explained how it worked from his side, the slaughter, in other words the warehouse where the stolen load would be taken to then distributed from, and options on how he would stage the hijacking or theft of the lorry and load. He reassured Dom that he would get his tractor and trailer back, but the tachograph would be smashed to conceal the distance the lorry had travelled after the heist.

Dom objected to Ian smashing the tacho as it would cost a small fortune to replace it. Dom thought, *What's more it belongs to my boss, and he won't be too pleased with the plan.* Ian agreed not to damage the unit or the trailer. It would be dumped on an industrial estate miles away from the slaughter and not to worry as it would soon be found. Chris focused on Titch and the crime squad questioning him and told him he would be stood up and questioned under pressure for two or three days because of the value. Then the conversation moved on to how to do it. Ian and Chris really showed their hand, and the verbals were captured on the recordings. They reassured Dom and Titch that they had done this many times in the past and identified loads, dates and the complicit haulage companies.

Dom knew this was good evidence to clear up previous crimes and add to their jail time. Ian and Chris suggested doing a spoof police stop, just a straight theft from a stop, or a Ministry of Transport check or staging a robbery by giving Titch a whack when he took a stop then nicking the load. Titch wasn't keen on the last option, although Dom laughed and voted for Titch taking a whack. Despite Dom's vote, it was agreed to go down as a simple theft with no violence involved. Once agreed, Ian explained how they would do the job.

"Titch will pick up the load from Scottish and Newcastle and take his usual route south and stop in the first layby after Barton Park truck stop at junction 56 on the A1(M). You can't miss it. Chris and my driver will be in convoy with you and pull in behind you. Get out of your truck and go and stand at the side, using the trailer to cover you from the passing traffic. My lad will come to you and just hand him the keys. You then make your way to Chris in the car. He will drive you around for a while and drop you off miles away. Got that so far?"

Titch nodded. Chris picked up the instructions. "I'm going to take you for about an hour or so. This is the important bit. You never saw anyone's face. They had stockings over their heads, and you were bundled into the back of a car between two fellas with a sack over your head. You tell the old bill you stopped for a piss, and they jumped you. Before you knew it you were on the ground, and they put a sack on your head. You didn't see any faces, that's double important and it will save you grief with the old bill and going through photograph albums. Got it, Titch?"

Titch, still nodding, asked, "Where will I get put out, and no rough stuff, right?"

Chris assured him. "Mate, why do we have to rough you up? You're on our side. Don't matter where I drop you, you'll have your phone and you call Dom and tell him what's happened. Dom calls the police, by which time the trailer is unloaded and the truck is left parked up to be found later. It's tried and tested, lads."

A few 'what ifs' were discussed by the four men, and it was agreed as soon as Dom got notice of the next run of booze he would call Chris and see if the timing worked for him. The meeting lasted about an hour, after which the two parties went their own way. Dom took his *Newcastle Chronicle* and supplement with him, together with the prize of Ian and Chris's verbals. Titch had played his role to the full and smiled at Dom as they walked back to the Merc. Ian and Chris crossed the motorway via the footbridge. Prior to getting into the car, Titch went to one side and shut off his device. Dom did the same in the car and gave Titch the thumbs up. Once reunited inside the Mercedes, they shook hands and laughingly complimented each other on their performances.

Titch said, "Walk in the fucking park, mate and what about those other jobs they have just coughed, fucking classic, mate. Another job down to Titch and Dom, the Manchester double act of haulage. We should be on stage in the West End."

"The stage?" Dom said then laughed. "Think big," he added.

"Like how big?" Titch said.

"Like as big as an Odeon cinema screen."

Cue more laughter.

Chapter 30: Mixed Feelings

At the following debrief, Terry had mixed feelings on hearing all that had happened. He now had to, or his team had to, dig through boxes of undetected crimes fitting the dates and circumstances of the additional disclosures made by Ian and Chris. They would need to find the offences and prepare their interviews to include them as well as the matter in hand. Ian, Chris and their criminal mates would be seeing a lot of jail time. However, Terry knew Dom had given them a big advantage in that they were now in control of when the lorry theft was going to take place. Ian and Chris were waiting for Dom's call, giving Terry and the team at least two days' notice. After completing the usual notes and exhibits, Dom and Titch started counting the ten grand. That done, Dom said farewell and headed for his hotel room. There, he packed his gear, including his mate Jameson, into his overnight bag and the tricky stuff into his holdall. Taking one last look around the hotel room, he turned around the Do Not Disturb sign to indicate to the chambermaid that the room was free to clean.

Before leaving Manchester, he had a trip down memory lane by driving onto the estate where he was dragged up. It was different. He was different. The gardens had not changed much, the odd knackered washing machine, sofa, rubbish sacks and of course the compulsory mattress. It had been decades since Dom had run around these streets with his mates and some of them still lived there, but Dom had nothing in common with them now and didn't bother looking them up. With a quick nostalgic pause outside his old council house, he drove back to his completely different life and environment that seemed a million miles away.

Once Terry had everything ready to go, he called Bob and gave him the day for the heist. Bob, in turn, called Titch and Dom to make sure the date was okay with them. "I'll put a call into Chris today, mate, and tell them Wednesday. What time do you want Titch to pull out of the brewery?" Dom said.

"We were thinking at around ten in the morning as that will give us a full day to play with them. I thought you and Titch could come on Tuesday, park the lorry overnight in South Shields and Titch could drive into the brewery on Wednesday morning, then if the bad guys are watching they will see him drive in and drive out later with the load," Bob said.

"Sounds like a plan, mate. Do you and Terry want to meet up with me and Titch at the Little Haven Hotel for a briefing on Tuesday evening?" Dom asked.

"I'll speak with Terry and get back to you Dom. Speak later, bye." Bob hung up.

Everyone involved in the operation was busy taking care of their area of responsibility. Titch was arranging to collect the truck and trailer from the covert haulage off-site location. A covert technical team had fitted an electronic surveillance device, a tracker, to the tractor unit to assist with the surveillance and the security of the valuable load. Terry liaised with his inside security contact at the brewery, making the final arrangements as well as managing the operational team, surveillance team and the arrest strategy. Dom had to contact Chris as soon as possible to confirm that Wednesday suited him and Ian. He also needed to confirm his man on the inside at the brewery knew which lorry and load to look out for. Dom drove to the industrial estate to get some background noise whilst he spoke with Chris. Dom told him he had a run on Wednesday if they fancied it. Chris didn't hesitate.

"We've been ready for the last few days, Dom, just waiting on you. Wednesday's good, mate. What time are we looking at?"

"Titch is tipping in Durham late on Tuesday. He will probably get into the yard, load and be out by half nine, ten o'clock."

"That's magic, Dom. I'll need to know the registration so my man can make sure he does the load." Dom gave him the registration, make, model and colour of the lorry Titch would be driving and hung up.

Chapter 31: Barton Park Services

Terry's operational plan included having his surveil-lance team parked up at Barton Park Services and wait for Titch to drive past on his way to the lay-by. The surveillance team would be monitoring Titch's route using the technical surveillance equipment. Terry was aware Ian and Chris were crooks, but they were no fools. They would probably have a third eye, some counter-surveillance, on their prize. Terry knew that conventional surveillance had to be minimal, and best leave it to the tracker. Once Titch had handed over the keys and the lorry was driven off, the tracking team would keep the lorry under control at a safe distance to not to show out to any third eye. The tracker car was crewed with a driver, a guy on a laptop giving distance, speed and location of the lorry and a guy in the back reading the maps. The activity in the tracking car would be hectic and noisy with the radio sending out information to the team, and the continuous beeping sound of the laptop as it picked up the signal from the tracking device. Then, there was the guy in the back reading the maps and using the radio to update the team behind them.

The conventional surveillance team who doubled up as the arrest team once the order was given to strike would stay a safe distance behind the tracker car, changing position and speed in their convoy to avoid the attention of a third eye. The strike would be called when the lorry was at the slaughter and all the players were busy unloading the booze. Terry didn't want Chris having the chance of getting on his toes, running away, or being together with Titch if any of the many moving parts went wrong. So, it was decided to use a second tracker and surveillance team to follow Chris and Titch. The tracking device would be secreted inside Titch's jacket. When the strike was called at the slaughter, Chris and Titch would be stopped and both nicked, playing out the subterfuge that Titch wouldn't know about it. The protests from Titch would be realistic. When Chris and Titch were arrested, they would be taken away in separate cars – Chris to a designated police station to enjoy his first of many nights behind bars and a meal provided by the police canteen. Titch would be taken back to the hotel for a couple of pints and a meal ordered from the à la carte menu.

On Tuesday evening Dom picked up Titch from the lorry park on the outskirts of South Shields and drove to the Little Haven Hotel where Terry, Dave and Bob turned up to brief them, together with two tech guys who took Titch's jacket to fit and test the tracking device. Terry went over the plan in detail. Dave was to stay around the brewery together with a couple of uniforms and when he got the word from Terry, he was to arrest the inside man with the assistance of the uniforms and Terry's brewery security contact. It was like a military operation; he had considered every possible scenario and what ifs. Dom commented that there were a lot of moving parts that could go wrong but was confident in Terry's ability to roll with the punches on the day. A lot had gone into this job, and no one wanted to be responsible for it going wrong. Once the briefing was over, Dom and Titch left to have a late dinner and a couple of pints at the bar. They retired to their beds at around eleven. As Titch was opening the door to his room, Dom told him to make sure he did not open his curtains in the morning butt naked. Titch looked puzzled as he disappeared into his room.

Chapter 32: Ian's Insider

The next day, Dom and Titch were up early and one of the first in for breakfast. It was no doubt going to be a long day, so they had the full monty: cereal, croissants, toast, and a full English breakfast after which Dom drove his mate back to the lorry park. Titch completed his normal daily checks on the truck and trailer, then fired up the engine. The tracking teams had activated the equipment on the tractor unit and in his jacket. Satisfied that the equipment was working, they switched it off and made their way to the service station where the two surveillance teams were waiting. Titch set off for the Scottish and Newcastle brewery. Dom drove to Bob's office where they could monitor the operation and Dom had his phone ready in case Ian or Chris called him.

Titch pulled up at the brewery gates, giving the gateman a reference number that Terry had given him at the briefing. This was an authorisation to collect a load. The security guy directed Titch to the appropriate loading area in the yard. Jumping down from the cab, Titch began to open the curtains on both sides of the trailer. As he was doing so, a guy approached him and addressed him by name. "Titch?"

This must be Ian's insider, he thought. "Yeah, that's me, buddy, are we good?"

"I'll get you loaded in a jiffy, mate, and back out on the road," the loader said.

Twenty minutes later, Titch handed a docket to the security guard on the gate who cleared him to leave. Titch and the load turned into the traffic. He knew that Chris was somewhere behind him but didn't waste any time looking for him in his mirrors. He had worked out it would take him about an hour to reach the lay-by. As he was passing the exit for Washington on the A1(M), he saw Ian standing on an overbridge. He immediately phoned Bob to let him know that the opposition had indeed deployed a third eye. Bob shared this valuable information with Terry, who in turn passed it on to the technical and conventional surveillance teams.

On approaching Barton Park service station, Titch called Bob to update him on his position and to give the surveillance teams the heads up and to fire up the equipment. A few minutes later, he pulled into a large lay-by.

Titch had just walked round the side of his lorry, shielding himself from the passing traffic, when Chris and another man approached him. "Good to see you, mate," Chris said. "Give me the keys." Titch took the keys from his pocket and the other guy took them from him.

Without a word, the stranger walked round to the front and climbed into the cab. Chris and Titch walked to Chris's car that was parked directly behind the trailer. Both vehicles pulled off in convoy. As soon as he could, Chris picked up speed, overtook the lorry, and headed south on the A1(M). Titch wondered what Chris would talk about on their mystery tour. He didn't have to wonder for too long. Chris filled most of the journey talking about his life of crime encompassing stolen lorry loads, drug dealing, enforcing, money lending and his role as Ian's right-hand man. To lighten the mood, Titch threw in a few funny stories about driving in Europe and some scrapes he'd had with the old bill in Manchester.

Meanwhile, the lorry and its load were heading back north on the A1(M). The unknown driver had driven south to the first exit and did a U-turn and was heading back to Newcastle with the load of booze. The technical surveillance team had good control of the load and the conventional team were finding it easy to hide amongst the heavy traffic. The lorry drove to a shabby looking storage warehouse on the northern outskirts of the city where a waiting accomplice opened two metal gates leading into a yard. The lorry drove into the yard and stopped by a roller shutter door which was opened from the inside. The driver and the gate keeper began to open the curtain sides on the trailer as a forklift truck appeared from the open roller door, driven by Ian Maloney.

A foot surveillance operative wearing a Hi-Vis jacket, a hard hat, and carrying a clipboard was pushing a click wheel, a wheel with long handles used by surveyors to measure distance. He walked by the gates measuring and randomly stopping to record his fictitious data. He informed the team using his covert radio what was going on in the yard and that subject one, Maloney, was unloading the trailer driving a forklift truck. Then he heard Terry's command over the radio, "Strike! Strike! Strike!"

It all kicked off. Cars screamed up to the yard, almost crashing into each other trying to get through the gate first to reach Maloney and his two mates. As this was going on Terry called the team following Titch to strike at the earliest opportunity. The message was received just as Chris was approaching the roundabout junction for Wetherby. Most of the surveillance team convoy had got themselves in a position behind Chris's vehicle but just before the roundabout, one of the team that was ahead of Chris's car blocked the access to the roundabout. The following cars then blocked him in from the side and rear. Chris and Titch were not going anywhere.

Titch shouted, "What the fuck!" But before he could say another word, he was pulled out of the passenger door at the same time Chris was pulled out of the driver's door. Titch was held down and handcuffed in full view of Chris. One of the cops read out Titch's rights. Then, Titch was pulled away and pushed into the rear of one of the cars used to make the stop. Chris was given the same treatment and put into the back of another vehicle and driven off. The whole drama was over in two minutes. Then Terry let the team know the insider had been arrested at work, soon to become his former workplace.

Bob and Dom made their way to the Little Haven and met Titch. The technical guys had recovered their tracker and Titch was nursing a bump on his head inflicted by his colleagues as they pulled him from the car. Dom took his mate Jameson from his bag and poured three small tots into some teacups. Bob politely declined the offer, so Dom shared Bob's ration between him and Titch who took a sip and grimaced. "Don't know what you like about this stuff, mate."

Raising his teacup, Dom offered a toast. "To Ian, Chris and the others, may your days be long and your nights lonely. Cheers Terry, good job."

By the end of the day the body count was five in the traps, the cells. Five house searches and a warehouse had been completed. Terry knew there would be more bodies and searches before this job came to court. Titch and Dom knew the chances of seeing Ian and Chris again were slim unless they gave it a run at court on a not guilty plea. That would not be in their best interests.

Chapter 33: Contract Killer

Sam's on the Scene

Here's the thing about contract killings, they can be tricky beasts. As a Senior Investigation Officer, managing a contract killing takes balls. You must protect the proposed victim and at the same time control the person who is intent on killing. Dom recalled sitting in a police station canteen with a young area Commander who was on the accelerated promotion path. He'd been asked to meet the Commander because of information that had been received from a snout, informant, that he'd been approached by a man who was looking for someone to kill someone on his behalf. This is what the undercover world would call a contract killing.

The area Commander asked Dom what courses of action were available to him in dealing with the threat to life. Dom went through the various options. He could go round to the house of the guy who was looking at placing the contract, knock on his door and tell him the police know what he's up to and tell him not to do it. It wouldn't be a smart move to nick him because that might blow the snout out and place him in danger, and what's more there wasn't any evidence to nick him. The snout is not going to give you a detailed five-page statement of the proposal, and it would be his word against the other. So, let's kick that idea into the long grass.

Another option would be to take the potential victim and his family into some sort of protective custody, almost like a witness protection program. But for how long and at what cost? Not practical. Into the long grass along with option one. Park a marked police car outside the potential victim's address. That wouldn't make the threat go away. It might just delay things. That can go with option one and two. You can go and have a chat with the potential victim and find out why this guy wants him dead. Not a good idea because it could lead to a tit for tat situation. We could get control of the contract using undercover officers, thereby securing evidence against the contract holder and lock him up.

The young Commander looked at Dom and asked, "What's the risk?"

Dom paused for a few seconds and pondered over the answer. "They all come with risk, boss, but we can risk assess and manage the risk at each step. The first thing to do is get control of the contract. Once we've got that we've got control of the potential victim and the arsehole that wants him dead."

"No, what's the risk to me? How and what am I exposed to?"

Dom didn't know what high-risk strategy the Commander opted for, but he didn't contact Dom again and he didn't hear of any unexplained or suspicious deaths in his command area. Dom guessed the potential victim and the snout lived to fight another day or their bodies had not yet been found.

Fortunately, not all contract killing jobs go that way. Dom was involved in a few contract killing jobs as the tactical advisor, sourcing and managing the undercover officers for the Senior Investigation Officer and his operational team. On other contracts he was deployed as the final undercover officer or one in the chain of officers deployed to move the job along to protect the potential victim and informant.

It all began as a normal day in the life of a busy cop who was wearing two, three or four hats at the same time. One of these hats was managing Operation Candle, which was going well. Dom had another moody lorry job on the go involving his mate from the Holiday Inn, which was progressing. Dom was also brushing up on his Spanish, *Dos cervezas, por favor*, in preparation for the final stage where everyone got nicked and the drugs seized, 'executive action stage' as the higher-ups liked to call it in their corporate speak.

Dom first got to know Sam on Operation Candle, an operation he was running. It was a unique undercover operation set up to counter an intelligence black hole in a large town in the middle of England. There was an area of the town known to be a hive of activity populated by an organised crime group. There were no informants on the ground. These criminals thought they were fireproof. Sam and another UCO called Phil were part of Dom's team. They were from different undercover units than Dom. He selected Phil and Sam because he had known about both UCOs from previous jobs when they had established themselves as top-drawer undercover officers. They had also attended specialist courses together. But 'known about' is way different than 'knowing.' So, rewind – Dom first got to know Sam on Operation Candle. The stars got to collide.

On Operation Candle, Dom, Sam and Phil devised a plan

to embed themselves in the community with Sam posing as a businesswoman operating an online lingerie, designer handbags and clothing business. Phil's cover story was an online business selling sports gear. With the help of a police technical support department, they got to work building websites, arranging covert personal and business bank accounts, credit cards, driving licences and passports.

At the outset, Dom said to Phil and Sam, "You never know, there could be some airmiles in this job." Little did he know, he was right. Operation Candle was an amazing 'bit of work.' It was also the catalyst that brought Dominic and Samantha together. Two alphas, two undercover officers, eventually living under the same roof. There were times on that operation they would engage in fierce rows, but no one knew it because as soon as they went to a briefing or debriefing, they turned into professionals used to putting on a false face. Sam would put away her flash bang eruptions and Dom acted like nothing had happened.

Somehow, and through that old black magic as the song says, and some would call it personal chemistry, a purely working arrangement transformed into an intimate relationship.

Dom already knew his marriage to Judy was in trouble and accepted the fault lay with him. Later, he would tell his kids he might not have been a good husband, but he always tried to be a good dad. The landlord of his local village pub who had run pubs in London close to one of the Flying Squad offices had a good comprehension of squad type officers and their mentality. He described Dom's lifestyle as that of an airline pilot. With hindsight, Dom came to understand what he meant. Dom was so focused on his job and the various undercover roles he didn't see the bleeding obvious in front of him.

Dom and Judy had drifted apart and were like ships passing in the night when he was home. They made the decision to stay together until their son, H, had finished his GCSE exams and was ready to move on to his A levels. They were honest with each other and accepted a breakup was never going to be easy. But they weren't doing each other any favours staying in the marriage. The kids knew what the future held. When Dom was home, he slept in one of the spare rooms. Social gatherings with friends had become a thing of the past.

Dom kept his home life private except he did talk about it with his boss, Major Crime head, Michael Palmer or MP as everyone called him. MP and Dom were having a few drinks after work one evening during the O'Toole contract killing deployment. That deployment took place after the start of Operation Candle and was a short-term gig as opposed to the long-term Op Candle saga. Possibly too much Jameson on Dom's part, but he felt relaxed and secure in MP's company, so he came clean about the state of his marriage. MP was a good listener as well as a good drinking partner. A sense of relief washed over Dom now that he had been honest with his boss about his home life.

Eventually the GCSEs were done, and Dom ventured out, searching for rented accommodation. He'd decided to find somewhere for six months to give him time to adjust and think through his future. He wanted to find somewhere close to work and close to the former matrimonial home for the sake of his children. He rented a converted farmhouse outbuilding. When the kids came to stay over for the first time, Dom's daughter, BB, described it as a robber's hideout. Nevertheless, Dom decided it would do for six months since he was still spending time away working... as usual.

News travels fast in any workplace and the undercover office was no different. Out of pity or an attraction to Dom's winning personality, he was inundated with support from colleagues and friends with many offers of Sunday lunch and nights out. Sam was but one who offered an invitation. After a debrief, the team were heading home or the robber's hideout in Dom's case. Initially, he was taken aback by Sam's offer of a quick drink but thought, *What harm is there in a quick drink?* The rest is history as they say.

Sam is mainly a bubbles, Sauvignon Blanc and a G&T girl with an odd red wine thrown in for good measure. Dom was a red wine, and occasional lager drinker, not forgetting his best mate in a bottle, Jameson. They had too much of all of them during the quick drink which wasn't quick at all. They shared a lot of personal anecdotes and banter and got on well. Neither of them was in a fit state to drive at closing time and decided to take a taxi to Dom's robber's hide out. It seemed natural to carry on chatting and have a nightcap. One thing led to another... and the rest is a case of what happened at the hideout, stays in the hideout.

The next morning, they took another taxi ride to where they had left their cars. The journey was totally silent. There was a frostiness in the air, a casual indifference which most people would recognise as the proverbial awkward silence. Dom certainly felt awkward but understood Sam's silence. They had crossed a line. But they dealt with it like two adult working professionals. On the day before their next Operation Candle briefing where all the team was to be present, they talked on the phone, mutually agreeing to keep their liaison to themselves. Once more and using their stock in trade, deception, they presented a united front in the team's presence.

163

In the weeks and months ahead, their relationship blossomed. Even so, they decided to keep their romance secret, only divulged to trusted friends and colleagues. They had no desire to supply ammunition to those who might question if they could work together and compartmentalise their private and operational lives. They were confident they could handle the situation without any third parties sticking their oar in. For third party, read nosy bastards.

Months passed by and the rental on the robber's hideout was ending so Dom found another place to rent. It was handy for the office and Sam's place. Inevitably, he started spending more time under Sam's roof. The relationship was now full on. Dom and Sam went on holiday together taking James, Sam's son and her mum and dad. Dom started doing the school run and covering childcare. He even did some DIY around Sam's house. It must have been love for he hated DIY. In the year that followed, Dom was splitting his time between his rented house and Sam's house until they had a long and serious conversation about him moving in lock stock and barrel. They both felt committed, so it happened... eventually.

Sam and James had been on their own for many years and there were a lot of adjustments to be made by all, but they worked through it and continued to work at it. As Sam reminded Dom constantly, "It was on the cards."

As Dom would say, "Sam, she who must have the last word."

But that's jumping ahead as long before they were in a relationship and despite their frequent clashes in the workplace, Dom brought Sam into the O'Toole contract killing operation whilst he, Phil and Sam were deployed on Operation Candle. Nothing unusual about that as an undercover officer often has several gigs on the go at the same time.

Chapter 34: Harold O'Toole

Billy from a covert unit in middle England rang Dom and, in his calm, low clipped middle class Scottish accent told him a story. He didn't interrupt. Billy needed at least three undercover officers today, not tomorrow, to take control of a contract to kill that was being touted around on his ground. He already had one of his undercover officers talking with the informant with the aim of arranging a sit down or further phone call with the contract holder today. Billy continued, "This guy's fucking weird, Dom. No previous, not on anyone's radar screens and I've checked with everyone, Customs, Box, NCIS – you name them, I've asked them. He goes by the name of Harold O'Toole. Other than his name, address, and phone number we know the square root of zero currently. Hopefully by the time you get up here with a team we'll know more. You are coming up with a team, Dom, are you not?"

He delivered his words in that slow talking gentle Edinburgh accent of his that could charm the birds out of the trees. How could Dom refuse? He owed Billy a favour from a year or so ago and today he was cashing in his credit note.

"Sounds like an interesting bit of work and quite the character, Billy. Give me half an hour and I'll get back to you, I will have to make a few phone calls. Bye for now, Billy boy."

"Aye, cheerio, Dom."

No time to waste, Dom's brain had already kicked into gear. First things first, where was he going to get a team of three UCOs at the drop of a hat? *Bingo!* His team of three would consist of Sam, Phil, and yours truly. Sam and Phil were part of Operation Candle, but Dom knew they had some downtime on that gig. Besides, Dom thought it would be good to work with Sam on another operation, seeing he felt they were getting to understand each other the more they worked together. Next step, speak with Mike Palmer, the boss, to get his support and let his two babies and him off the plot for a day. Dom punched MP into the phone index and pushed the green call button. Mike Palmer was known by all as just MP.

"Hi boss, can you talk?" Dom said using the usual phrase that meant he wanted to speak to him about something confidential. The tone in his voice suggested it was something urgent.

"Yes, since about the age of three, Dom. Have we got a problem, mate?" Dom loves MP's sense of humour.

"No, no problem, boss," Dom said as he ran out Billy's story, ending with the idea of using the three amigos from Operation Candle. He did dress it up a bit by telling MP they could use their absence from the plot as a bit of theatre. Theatre is a phrase used to describe a bit of stage dressing or a diversion carried out by the UCOs on the plot for the benefit of the targets. The team set the scene and the target sees or hears what is laid out in front of him and her and walks into it. It's like watching a stage production being played out. Phil and Sam could put it around the plot later today they had dropped on to an end of line bit of stock going cheap up North, so they were off early tomorrow morning. That's a good example of theatre.

166

Dom, naturally, would have Billy forward MP a formal request, a MOU (Memorandum of Understanding) and the signed back page of the authority. All to be sent to MP by secure email to satisfy the management that the operation was fully authorised. Dom would do the same for Phil and Sam's units.

"Is that the same Billy that gave us the two girls for the night club job a while back, soft spoken Jock?" MP said.

"Yeah, you've got him, boss. A good lad, I'd like to help him out with your blessing. My thoughts are to get a flier in the morning. Phil and Sam can make their own way there in their van so if things drag on, they can vacate and get back here under their own steam and Taff from the office can cover in my absence. I'll drive up in my car with an overnight bag. How's that sound as a bit of a plan, boss?"

"Sounds like you're working off the back of a fag packet, mate."

"In a way, yes. This is all a bit of a rush job," Dom said.

MP finished the call by saying, "All right, make sure the paperwork gets here and to the other two's offices before you go on the pavement, and keep in touch. Good luck. See you soon, mate."

Now for Phil's and Sam's office. No resistance from either. They knew Dom and Billy and trusted them to look after their merchandise and return it to them in mint condition. They insisted on all the paperwork being with them before any deployment took place and quite right.

Chapter 35: Sambush

D om picked up his phone to call Billy. It was exactly twenty-two minutes since Dom put the phone down on him asking for half an hour to sort things out. Billy answered the phone before Dom heard a ring tone at his end.

"Hello, Dom, are we good to go?" It was that slow, soothing, calm accent of his. Dom wondered what Billy's heart rate was. He'd guess his resting heart rate was no more than forty-two beats per minute – pretty slow.

"Yes, mate, we're good to go. I've got Phil and Sam coming up to help. They're doing a bit of work for me at the mo so it wasn't too hard to get hold of them. You know them both by different names." Dom gave Billy their units and Billy confirmed he knew both and had worked with them separately on previous occasions. Dom also gave Billy details of Phil and Sam's offices and reminded him their management was expecting the relevant paperwork to be sent across, as did his boss, asap. He then gave Billy their National Undercover Numbers which identified them on the National UC Register. He would need them for the authority, MOU and request.

"What time do you need us with you tomorrow, mate?" Dom said.

"Oh, let me think for a wee minute, pal. If you can come to

our off-site for, shall we say nine o'clock tomorrow morning that would be perfect, Dom."

Dom laughed before saying, "Fucking hell, Billy, do you ever change up a gear or get excited about anything and what is your resting heart rate, fella? Nine o'clock at your place mate, it's a date. Don't forget to get that paperwork out to everyone please."

"I will, Dom, and thanks for your help. What's my resting heart rate got to do with anything?"

"Nothing mate, I'll catch you tomorrow morning. Bye, mate."

"Cheerio, Dom."

Now to tell Phil and Sam of the new plan. This would be best done face to face, so Dom called Sam. He was aware that it pissed Sam off if he called Phil as first point of contact all the time. This first came to notice at an early Operation Candle debrief when Sam asked him if he had her burner phone number in his covert phone. Dom sensed there was a sting in the tale about to happen. It was more like an ambush which Dom later renamed as a Sambush.

"Yeah, of course I have. What's that all about?"

"Well, you might want to try ringing me first now and then instead of Phil all the time when you have something to say. Just saying." She finished the Sambush off with an over exaggerated smile, leaving Dom with a feeling he had been the recipient of a deserved kick in the bollocks.

"Point made, Sammy." Dom knew the use of Sammy wouldn't land well with her but he had to get the last shot in. Or try to.

"Please, Sam or Samantha, Dom...in...ic," she said, elongating the pronunciation of Dominic and knowing his preference was Dom. She must have the last word. Since that day Dom always alternated who he called first.

Dom rang Sam's phone which rang for some time. He was just about to leave her a message and then call Phil when she picked up. "Sorry, Dom, I was on the loo, is everything okay?"

Too much information, Dom thought. "Yeah fine, are you all right to talk?" A clear signal he wanted to talk about cop stuff.

"Yeah, we're in the flat designing some leaflets we are having printed off. What can we do for you?"

"I need a meeting at the café in the next hour, please. Got a change of itinerary coming up. Does an hour work for you two?"

"Yep, see you there in an hour. Bye." Short and sweet response, but that was Sam.

They had a few locations they would use for meetings between the three of them and a cover story in place in case someone came in and recognised Phil or Sam. The café was a posh place by the river and was Dom's preferred meeting place. He enjoyed the view, and the clientele were mainly retired couples. It was a secluded location a good distance from the plot.

Phil and Sam were sitting at an outside table on the decking with three cups of coffee on the table. Phil and Dom always greeted each other with a strong handshake and a peck on the cheek for Sam. She always smelt good and looked good with expensive perfume and stylish clothing.

"Okay, mate, share this change in itinerary with us," Phil said.

Dom loved Phil. He was a different type of character to him. He had the look of an Eastern European gangster. But as soon as he greeted you his gentle and attractive personality flooded out.

You could not help but instantly warm to him. His personality was ideal for Operation Candle, which was temporarily on the back burner, so Dom put them both in the picture.

"Billy from the shires has been on the phone. He's got a contract job come into him and is looking for a team of three on the hurry up to get control of the contract and lock up the bad guy. I've suggested us three, if you fancy it. It will be a quick in and out for you two, moving the job on to yours truly. If you fancy it, we need to be at Billy's off-site at nine tomorrow morning. I've got the okay from both of your management and the paperwork is on the way to them as we speak."

Phil and Sam looked at each other and quickly discussed what they had planned for the next day. They decided nothing would spoil if it was to slip a day or two. Dom told them his idea of a cover story about getting a good deal on some stock up north and how they might use that on the plot as a bit of theatre and to enhance their business interests and profile. With all three amigos singing off the same song sheet, they finished coffee over some small talk about nothing.

Just before they went their separate ways, Sam said, "If we're going to collect some stock, we'll have to go up in the Transit van, Phil, rather than the Jag. That's not good, darling."

Dom said, "The van's fine. Sam, it's not like you're driving the length of the country in it."

Phil chipped in. "Dom, it's fine if it's not raining but your feet get piss wet if you're sat in the passenger seat and it rains."

"Best you drive then, Phil," Dom said with a touch of sarcasm and knowing Phil would rather drive his Jaguar.

Sam responded by blowing kisses in Dom's direction. "Piss off, I'll jump in with you Dom if Phil takes the van, sweetie. We can meet up at the motorway service at seven and I'll get in your Merc with you, darling."

They laughed and agreed to Sam's amended plan.

Chapter 36: Operation Lamplight

The following morning they didn't hang around at the service station as time and traffic was against them. Phil grabbed three takeaway coffees and handed them out. Sam jumped into Dom's Mercedes and blew a kiss at Phil who gave her the bird in return.

Billy was waiting in the office and buzzed them in on arrival. The kettle was going, and the brew kit, milk and stained mugs were available on the table next to it. Billy introduced Freddie to the gang of three. Freddie was a recent addition to the National Register and was the first UC in on this job. Billy rolled out his plan and filled in the up-to-date intelligence picture.

"The subject of the operation is a sixty-five old man by the name of Harold O'Toole. He's a retired, well off, nondescript individual who lives alone in an expensive house in a nice residential part of town. He's a member of a local ballroom dancing group that meets once a week in the nearby village hall to practice their moves and shapes. The group travel nationally at weekends to compete in competitions against like-minded people. He has no criminal history, hence no trace on PNC. The only additional information we have currently on the victim has come from a phone call between Freddie, who is using the name Frankie on the job," Billy nodded towards Freddie, "and

O'Toole last night. The potential victim is one of three men that attends the same dance group as O'Toole. These three guys also attend a sports centre together every Wednesday evening to use the gym. They jog to and from the gym come rain or shine."

At this point, Dom was unable to resist a bit of storytelling, but it was for a good reason. Dom always felt it was part of his job by educating other less experienced UCOs through his anecdotes. He said, "It's always good practice and tradecraft to use the pseudonym of a UC even if you know his real name and you are in a safe environment. It makes it easier on the plot and lessens the chance of calling someone by the wrong name in the presence of the opposition. I recall some years back I was pulled in on a job and met another UCO for the first time at a meeting. I introduced myself to the guy. And it went something like this. 'Mate, hi, I'm Dom,' I said as the guy held out his hand. The other UCO responded in a strong Welsh accent, 'Hello, boyo. I'm Dafydd.' Without thinking I said, 'What's your real name, mate?' He snapped back at me sounding like Windsor Davies from the excellent TV programme *It Ain't Half Hot Mum*, 'That is my real fucking name.' It was a bumpy start to a working relationship, but we became good friends inside and outside the job. Sorry, Billy. I didn't mean to interrupt."

"No worries, mate. I love that story, as I was saying..." Billy continued with the briefing. "O'Toole has suggested to Frankie that he could point the victim out to him at the gym. Frankie has told O'Toole he will be back in touch with him later today. That's where we are, team. The Major Crime team have narrowed down and identified the three potential victims by discreet enquires with the chairperson of the dance group. They also went in on the back of a made-up moody story about a suspicious vehicle in and around the village hall over the last few days. The team obtained a list of all members of the dance group for the purpose of eliminating them from the enquiries. O'Toole features on that list with sixteen other men.

"Further moody enquiries around a suspicious motor with the local sports centre covering Wednesday. The centre operates CCTV which covers most areas including the car park and reception. All members use an electronic swipe system using a membership card to enter the centre. The CCTV shows three men jogging into the gym and leaving together about an hour later. The team have seized the CCTV and a printout of people swiping in from opening time to closing time on Wednesday. That's how they have identified the three men from the dance group. The Major Crime team are handling the enquiries and backgrounds on the three guys."

Dom butted in. "That's good old bill, nice to hear, but what brief have they been given when questioning these three guys, one of whom is the potential victim? We don't want to spook them, or this guy O'Toole getting a sniff of police involvement."

"Exactly, Dom, that is why I want to move really quickly on this bit of work. I want to do it like the old bust buy tactic. This guy isn't a career criminal and I think we can get him and the contract under control in three back-to-back moves. Freddie, I should say Frankie, has already had phone contact with O'Toole and O'Toole is waiting for a call with the next move. I want to pull O'Toole into a meeting today at some time with one of you three, and if it feels right bounce him into another UCO and finally into the person that's going to do the killing for him. Bit like those drug buys we used to do back in the day. This guy has no experience of covert tactics and apart from wanting to kill someone, he's a complete law-abiding citizen. The main thing is to get this contract under our control."

Billy told them by the time they got to the next briefing there should be more info and they could check out the details then and fine tune a strategy to deal with Mr O'Toole. He confirmed all the paperwork had been completed and received by the appropriate offices and a briefing with the SIO had been arranged in a hotel room at eleven o'clock.

Dom thought, *Billy has been busy, and probably not had much sleep. But he's still running at forty-two bpm.*

"What's this op called, Billy?" Dom asked.

"Lamplight. Don't ask me why, some intel guy at HQ pulls them off a list. I don't know if they're in alphabetical order or just random words, but that's it. Lamplight."

Chapter 37: Perfect Shot

Billy and Freddie, aka Frankie, travelled to the hotel together. Sam, Phil and Dom travelled in the Mercedes, leaving the van at the off-site.

On entering the hotel room, the SIO introduced himself as Graham Day and introduced them to his DI, Nick Brown, and a DS Paul Hindley. Dom had worked with Paul Hindley before. He was a good practical forward-thinking cop.

After doing the introductions and everyone had settled down, the SIO informed them there had been a significant development in the intelligence and asked Billy if he and Paul could have a conversation downstairs in private. The remaining undercover team thought nothing of this as they knew Graham Day, the SIO, and his team were utterly professional. Nothing more needed to have been said to the undercover officers gathered in the room. They knew whatever was to be discussed was of an operational nature and not for everyone's ears. No offence was taken.

The briefing got started after they returned to the room. The next half hour was taken up with issuing Pocket Notebooks (PNB), recording equipment and tapes. Billy had been to the local superstore and a couple of phone shops and purchased four throw away phones that would be used exclusively on this bit of work. He had even punched each individual phone number into three of the phones. The fourth phone had the number of Dom's throw away in the memory. All they had to do was to put a name to each number and they had their own private communication network. The boss gave them the official briefing which each UCO entered in his or her PNB and it was signed off by the boss. A photograph of O'Toole was produced. It was clearly a photograph taken from an observation post, OP. It was a clear picture of O'Toole walking down the footpath of a house towards the road. Dom thought, *Congratulations to the photographer. I know how difficult it can be to capture that perfect shot when you've been sweating your nuts off in the back of a van for hours. I was the worst photographer in the land. I don't think I took one picture that was in focus. This photograph could give David Bailey a run for his money.* Each UCO studied the photograph of O'Toole and burnt the image into their memory banks. Every officer signed to the effect that they had seen a photograph of O'Toole.

The agreed plan was for Frankie to call O'Toole and arrange a meeting outside the Hilton Hotel close to the motorway at three o'clock that afternoon. He was to tell O'Toole he would be met by a female who would take care of him and his business. The female would have long blonde hair, be wearing a long black coat, and reading a *Vogue* magazine. She would be there at precisely three o'clock. If he wasn't there by five past three, she would leave, and the deal was off.

Sam, the blonde reading *Vogue*, was to greet O'Toole on his approach and simply check it was him by asking for his name. Once confirmed, she was to ask O'Toole if he had come alone, ensuring no one else knew he was there. Then she was to ask him if he'd been followed and make sure no one was waiting for him in the car park. Once satisfied with O'Toole's replies, she was to tell him that if he wished to continue, he was to follow her into the hotel reception where she would introduce him to a friend.

Phil would be sitting alone at a table in a quiet corner of the hotel coffee lounge. Sam would then escort O'Toole to the table and say, "This is Mr O'Toole," and leave the hotel.

Phil would ask the same preliminary questions as Sam to display how professional and careful their outfit was. He would ask one further supplementary question: "Are you sure you want to go through with this? You can walk away at any time. It's your choice, Mr O'Toole." Providing he didn't back out Phil would tell O'Toole that he was going to leave and the man who would conduct the business on his behalf would join him directly. Phil would then leave the hotel.

At this stage, Dom would join O'Toole at the table, introducing himself as the man who would finalise the contract on his behalf for fifty thousand pounds. They knew this guy could afford it and didn't want to look cheap and unprofessional. Dom would then ask for half the money at the next meeting and the other half on completion of the contract. During all this, Dom would allow O'Toole to make the running and if he indicated he was having reservations, Dom would walk away and not attempt to change O'Toole's mind. The target must remain in the driving seat and exercise his own free will. This had to be O'Toole's decision. If everything went to plan, Dom would hand O'Toole the fourth throw away phone containing Dom's number. He would explain to O'Toole the strict rules that the phone could only be used to contact Dom and if he had to add call credit, he was to purchase it with cash only. He mustn't use a credit card or debit card to top up the phone. It was also stressed he must not use it to call anyone else other than Dom and not to share the number with anyone.

"That's the strategy, team. Any questions or suggestions?" asked Billy.

Chapter 38: The Famous Mob Hitman

The room all agreed that it sounded spot on and doable. It gave the impression that O'Toole was hiring a professional team who knew their craft. It was important to give O'Toole opportunities to pull out at any time. If the UCOs were to drive the job it could be argued later in court that the police acted as an agent provocateur.

Billy then gave them the opportunity to pick names they would use on the plot. "Freddie is using Frankie, very creative," said Billy.

Dom always tried to pick a name that had some tentative connection with the nature of the operation, so he said, "I'm using Joe as in Joseph Barboza, the famous mob hitman."

"Playing your silly little game again, Dom. Put me down as..." pausing for a while, Sam said, "Mary as in Mary and Joseph. See, you've now got me playing your stupid game."

Phil stood up and as he walked towards the bathroom, said, "I'll be Lou, work it out for yourselves."

So, Joe, Mary and Lou were now fully signed up to Operation Lamplight, together with Frankie.

The briefing broke up but before Dom left, he asked Billy for a private word. Once alone, Dom said, "What's the significant development all about? Can you tell me?"

Billy smiled. "Has that been running on a loop in the back of your brain since then?"

"Not really running on a loop, mate, but professional curiosity, shall we say," Dom said.

Billy continued, "One of the enquiry team had come up with some info about O'Toole. The boss wanted to bottom it out one hundred percent before deciding what to do with it or to share it with you and the team. As it turned out it wasn't our Mr O'Toole and came to nothing. Mistaken identity, mate."

Dom understood and made his way out to join the other UCOs at their cars outside. After the briefing and the tactical plan had been agreed each UCO left the room with their recording device and sat in the car and made their introductions on the tape. It's important for PII purposes that officers do not talk on each other's tapes when making introductions. Once the tape is on, all small talk and piss taking stops. The tape recording could be disclosed and played in a courtroom. Dom sat in his car to do the introduction after Sam and Phil had done theirs. He placed a new tape into the recording device and switched it on. First stating the time and date, he said, "I am a serving police officer in the United Kingdom and for the purpose of this operation I wish to be known as Joe. I have just placed a new tape into this device for a deployment I will be having later today where I will be meeting with a man I know as Harold O'Toole, who is looking for someone to kill a person on his behalf. I will now switch this device off until a time closer to the meeting and it is safe to switch on. The time now is still 12:30 on the same day." Dom turned off the device and put it away for safe keeping until it was time to engage with Mr Harold O'Toole.

Freddie took himself off to Billy's car and activated his recording device. Once the time and date statement was done, he said, "I'm just going to put a phone call in to Harold O'Toole." Pressing the last number dialled on his burner phone he waited for O'Toole to answer.

In an upper-class English accent, the voice on the other end said, "Hello. Harold here, how can I help you?"

"It's me, Frankie. I've got a meeting set up for three o'clock this afternoon if you are still serious about what we spoke about."

"Oh, hello Frankie. Yes, I'm still looking for someone to help me out and I can do three o'clock, depending on how far I have to travel."

"You know the Hilton Hotel just off the motorway on the northbound?"

"Yes, the junction just after that awful service station, yes I know it."

"Be there at precisely three o'clock, you'll see a blonde woman in a black coat reading a *Vogue* magazine outside. Go up to her and tell her your name. She'll take it from there. If you are not there by five past three, she will leave and the job's off. Is that clear?"

"Yes, perfectly clear. I'll be there bang on three, Frankie."

"Now listen, this is important. Don't tell anyone where you are going. Don't bring anyone with you. Drive yourself and don't have someone waiting in a car. Make sure you're not followed. These people are professional and will be monitoring you. Do you understand, Harold?"

"Yes, I completely understand. I'll be there at three, Frankie."

Freddie aka Frankie killed the call, then stated the time for the purpose of the tape and switched off the device. He returned to the hotel room and completed his PNB. Taking the tape from the device, he marked it as an exhibit and placed it in an evidence bag which he sealed ready to hand over at his debrief. The debrief was short and sweet and the admin was completed. In his West Midlands accent, Freddie commented on O'Toole's accent. "That fella talks like a member of the fucking Royal Family, and I don't mean those scousers off the telly, I mean Charlie and that lot. Strange fella, strange, strange fella."

Dom was to find out how strange Mr Harold O'Toole was.

Chapter 39: Camel Coat

By the time two o'clock had arrived, everyone was fed and watered with their game heads on. The boss had been busy on the phones arranging the surveillance at the hotel. He wanted to smudge the meetings, obtaining evidence by way of photographs, possibly video, of the meetings between O'Toole and the undercover officers.

Sam had popped out to the shops and bought the latest edition of *Vogue* and a family sized bag of liquorice allsorts. She burst into the room with the bag held high above her head. "This will keep our blood sugar levels up, guys." Sam knew that Phil and Dom weren't big fans of liquorice, therefore she was always going to munch the lion's share.

Freddie was to travel with Billy and wait at the services in case they were needed. Dom, Phil and Sam left early in the Mercedes. On arrival at the hotel, they left the Mercedes separately with a gap of a few minutes to set up in and around the hotel reception and coffee lounge. By two forty-five they were all in position, other than Sam who was sitting in the reception area until at five to three she went outside with her *Vogue* magazine. The surveillance team were good. Dom didn't notice anyone who looked out of place. Settling in, they reactivated their recording devices by making it look like they were using their mobile phones to mask they were dictating the time, date, and location for the benefit of the tape.

At precisely three o'clock a white male aged around mid-sixties arrived outside the hotel. He was smartly dressed in a brown camel coat, beige corduroy trousers and highly polished brown shoes, wearing a trilby hat, an open neck shirt and a cravat. He was carrying a leather satchel over his shoulder. Sam instantly recognised him as O'Toole from the photograph. This well-presented man did not look like a killer but looks sometimes deceive. He had seen the blonde carrying her copy of *Vogue*.

"Hello, my name is Harold O'Toole. I have an arrangement to meet a lady here at three o'clock today, I'm sorry I didn't get her name. Might it be you?"

"Yes, it is. Hello Mr O'Toole, or do you prefer Harold?"

O'Toole moved closer into Sam's space. "Call me Harold, please."

"Okay, Harold. Did you travel here alone?"

"Yes."

"Does anyone know you are here?"

"No."

"Is anyone waiting for you in the car park?"

"No."

"Do you think you have been followed here?"

Removing his hat, he replied, "No, I don't believe I've been followed. Is Frankie here?"

"No. Frankie's not here. Would you like to speak to him? You can call him if you want to."

"No, no, no, no, that's fine, I was just wondering. He sounded like a very nice chap on the phone. Let's get on, if we may."

"Thank you, Harold. If you wish to continue, please follow me into the hotel and I will introduce you to a friend who will be pleased to help you."

Sam turned and walked towards the automatic sliding doors leading into the hotel reception and lounge area. She heard O'Toole's footsteps following. Phil, aka Lou, was sitting in the far corner at a table with four chairs arranged around it. Striding confidently, Sam walked directly towards Lou. Sam stopped at the table and O'Toole stopped by her side. "This gentleman is Harold. I will leave him with you. Goodbye, Harold, it's been a pleasure to meet you."

"Yes, likewise. Sorry, I didn't get your name."

"Mary."

O'Toole continued, "Mary, goodbye Mary, maybe we'll meet again. I would look forward to it."

Mary turned to walk away. She left through the automatic doors and strode into the car park with O'Toole watching her until O'Toole heard Lou. "Hello, Harold. please take a seat and make yourself comfortable. I hope you don't mind but I have a few questions for you. I apologise if you have been asked these questions a few minutes ago but you understand we have to be very careful in our line of work."

"Yes, of course. Please ask away."

Lou leaned across the table towards O'Toole. "Does anyone know you are here today, Harold?"

"No. Well, that's not strictly true. Mary and Frankie know I'm here and of course you do."

Lou smiled politely. "Yes, of course. Did you travel here alone? Is anyone waiting for you?"

"No. I drove myself here and I don't believe I was followed."

Lou leaned back. "Excellent, Harold. Can I ask you to sit

here for a few moments and a very good friend of mine by the name of Joe will be with you directly? Please make yourself comfortable."

Lou walked away. O'Toole stood and watched Lou disappear into the reception area. Before O'Toole sat again, he removed the satchel from his shoulder, then took off his coat to reveal a waistcoat that matched the colour of his outer coat. Placing his coat and satchel on the vacant seat next to him, he noticed a man sitting with his back to him a few tables away. He seemed to be talking into a mobile phone held to his ear. Then the man stood and walked towards O'Toole. Within seconds the man was holding out his hand. "Hello, my name is Joe, my friend Lou has just spoken to me on the phone, and I believe you like to be called Harold?"

As he shook Dom's, aka Joe's, hand, O'Toole said, "Hello, Joe, yes I prefer Harold."

Dom felt O'Toole's soft and weak handshake. There was no strength nor any motion in the greeting. It was limp by any standard. Dom was immediately intrigued by his demeanour and style of dress, both at odds with his mission. He now understood what Freddie meant by 'strange, strange fella.' Dom let go of the limp hand and moved to the seat vacated by Lou.

Dom invited O'Toole to sit. "Please take a seat, can I get you a drink of anything?"

"Yes, please. I'll have some sparkling water with ice, thank you."

Chapter 40: Strange, Strange Man

Dom caught the attention of one of the waitresses who were busy buzzing round the lounge and ordered two bottles of sparkling water with ice. As they waited for the drinks to arrive, Dom didn't want to get into a detailed conversation about the contract, so he took the opportunity to satisfy his growing curiosity about this strange, strange man. "I hope you don't mind me saying, Harold, but you don't look, talk or dress like the people I usually work for. No offence meant... just curious."

O'Toole looked right into Dom's eyes and for a second, Dom saw the evil bastard behind the respectful and educated veneer. The hairs on the back of his neck sprang to attention in the vacuum of silence that hung over them for what felt like an eternity.

O'Toole broke the silence. "What is the idiom, Joe? You can't judge a book by its cover. Things or people are not what they appear to be at first glance, Joe."

The water arrived and Dom settled back. "Please, Harold, tell me how I can help you."

Sitting in the comfort and warmth of the Hilton Hotel lounge, O'Toole began to put his cards on the table, one by one. He was cold, calculated, and emotionless. "Joe, there is a female friend of mine by the name of Jean, who I long for. I want to take what is currently a social and friendly relationship to a long term, intimate and loving partnership. I feel... no, not feel, I know she has the same desires for me. We are both members of the same ballroom dancing group and spend time together at practice and when we travel away for competitions. The fly in the ointment is her husband, Terry. While he is still around Jean can't show her true feelings for me. This Terry character, her bloody husband, is in the same ballroom dancing group. He's always in the way, holding her hand, sitting next to her in the pub, staying overnight in hotels with her. I can't have any quality time with Jean. I can't get near her because he's round her like a bad smell all the time. I hate it. I hate him. I've been thinking about this for some time, and he must go. I want him dead, buried and out of the way forever. That's who and why I want to wipe this inconvenience off the face of the planet for me and Jean."

Dom didn't interrupt O'Toole as he told his tale. He saw and heard the change in tone and facial expression as each word was articulated. His eyes drilled into Dom's eyes with every word and his mouth snarled as he spat out his last. This man was truly evil and could kill in cold blood within the blink of the eye, Dom believed.

Chapter 41: Coiled Spring

Dom also knew he had to make sure he got control of this contract before O'Toole took it upon himself to take care of business in his own way and time. O'Toole was like a coiled spring under pressure, raring to release the tension pressing down on it. Dom had a game plan; he was working to an agreed strategy. He wanted O'Toole to believe he was hiring a professional, someone as cold and evil as he was. He wanted to dive straight in and say, *I'll do it, I'm your man. Look no further, Harold, I'll kill him for you.* Instead, Dom remained expressionless and unfazed by this story of love and hate.

Dom nodded to express he understood, then said, "These things take time, research, planning and money. Three of those components, time, planning, and research are my responsibility. The money is yours. My fees are the same for you as for everyone. If we decide to go forward with this business arrangement my fee is fifty thousand pounds. I will require half of the fee, twenty-five thousand pounds, when I agree to carry out the contract, and the other half on completion of the work. Is that acceptable to you?"

O'Toole did not blink at the figure or hesitate in his reply. "Yes, the money is no problem, worth every penny to rid me of this man. I have a history in finance and property and know the value of services and commodities, although my experience in this type of contract is very limited. Fifty K is acceptable."

Dom continued, "While we are talking about finances, let me give you my first bit of advice. How you amass the money. Don't draw it directly from your accounts in one or two hits. That may attract attention to yourself if you start a relationship with Jean soon after the contract has been filled. Find a way of gathering the money without leaving a trace. Do you understand the importance of what I'm saying?"

Picking up his satchel, O'Toole placed it on his lap as he said, "I'm a man of means, Joe. I have undisclosed and untraceable cash in a safe deposit box. I recently sold some land I inherited to a member of the travelling community. He was happy for two-thirds of the deal to go through the official channels and pay me the outstanding balance in cash. A win-win situation. So, thank you for the advice, but I'm already one step ahead."

"Good," Dom replied.

O'Toole opened the satchel and produced a buff folder. Placing the folder on the table, he gently pushed it towards Dom. Tapping on the folder he said, "Everything you need to know about Terry is contained in here. Photographs, address, place of work, phone number, routine, everything. I've been compiling this dossier for a long time. I'm sure you will be impressed with the detail."

Dom picked it up and gave the contents a quick once over page by page. He wasn't reading the typed material on the individual sheets or studying the photographs that had been stapled to sheets of A4 paper. Rather, he was thinking how meticulous O'Toole has been in his quest to eliminate Terry so he could have a life ever after with Jean. Dom had been engaged in many undercover operations and roles and met some nasty, violent, undesirable individuals. But looking across the table at O'Toole, Dom knew the man's inner core was evil, hiding behind an exterior of the nice older man who lives next door to your mother.

"Thank you, Harold, this looks very good and comprehensive. I will take it away with me and study the detail later in private if you decide to progress to the next stage. I said there were four points to consider. One was the money and we have agreed on that. The next stage is research. This file will assist me in this stage, thank you. I will use it to carry out my surveillance. This will take time, and the third point is that I will not be rushed. To do this we have to be patient and attention to detail is paramount and non-negotiable, as you have been in the preparation of this dossier. Once I have completed my research, I will plan the execution of the contract. Are you agreeable to this?"

Looking across the table, O'Toole's facial expression changed. It was back to that nice man who lives next door to you in the suburbs. He smiled at Dom. "Sounds perfect. I can have half of the money with you later today if that's what you would like."

This was strong evidence that he was serious. He was beating the drum and setting his own pace, without any help from anyone. Dom knew he had to control the situation by slowing the pace down so that the SIO could plan a strategy without O'Toole becoming impatient with him and taking the contract elsewhere. He needed to think fast. The answer was right in front of him. Before Dom spoke, he took the mobile phone, the one Billy had given to him prior to the deployment, from out of his jacket pocket and placed it nonchalantly on the table next to the buff folder. "Harold, I will take this folder away with me and study it. I will do some initial reconnaissance of my own over the next few days and I will be in touch with you via the phone I've just placed on the table. This phone has one number in its memory, my number. This is the only way you will communicate with me. The phone has no history. If you need to put credit on the phone pay for it with cash. Do not use a credit or debit card. Do not use a store loyalty card to collect points when you use cash. In short, Harold, do not connect this phone to you in any way. This is ultra-important."

O'Toole went to pick up the phone, but Dom stopped him. "Just leave the phone there for now, Harold. We have one more thing to agree on. At the end of this meeting and we shake hands the contract belongs to me. That means that you do not go looking for someone else to carry out the work. You do not place the contract with a third party, it belongs to me. Should you wish to pull out and have a change of heart or you are not satisfied with my timescale or performance, all you have to do is tell me and we shake hands and walk away. Is that clearly understood, Harold?"

O'Toole's facial expression had changed again. Now, he had the look of a determined and focused individual. "I understand completely about the phone and the exclusive ownership of the contract. You have my word as a gentleman."

Thinking, Dom ran through a mental check list of any other points he should raise with O'Toole. Satisfied he'd done a good job so far, Dom reached across the table and offered O'Toole his right hand.

He took up the invite and cupped Dom's hand in both of his as if he was thanking someone for a charitable act. Dom was surprised to find his grip was stronger than their earlier exchange. "Joe, thank you for taking this on. I will be always grateful to you. Trust me, I will not utter a word to anyone," he said, then released Dom's hand.

"I estimate the whole contract will be completed within two to four weeks from today, depending on my reconnaissance and surveillance. I will call you on that phone, which you can now pick up and keep safe, in the next few days. The next time we meet I will have a comprehensive update for you, and you will have twenty-five thousand pounds in used notes, non-sequential numbers for me. Agreed?"

Smiling again, O'Toole picked up the phone and put it away in his satchel. "Excellent, will we meet here, Joe?"

"I'll inform you on the phone, Harold. Goodbye for now." Dom collected the folder from the table and walked towards the exit as O'Toole finished off his sparkling water. Dom was confident that the whole meeting had been smudged by the operational team and the three amigos, he, Phil and Sam, had done a good job for Billy and the SIO. Dom also knew that the operational surveillance team would follow O'Toole from the hotel for any additional information and evidence.

Once back in his Mercedes and out of the sight and hearing of the public, Dom said the time out loud for the benefit of the tape and deactivated the recording device. He made his way back to the debriefing location, the same hotel room used for the briefing. He was the last to arrive. Phil was the first to greet him as he opened the hotel room door. "Hi, Dom, how'd it go?"

"Yeah, it went well. The guy's a nutter, mate, proper nutcase."

Chapter 42: Jekyll and Hyde

S am was sitting in a small chair at the dressing table reading *Vogue*, having already completed her notes and exhibits. Phil was just finishing off his bits and pieces. The SIO, Graham Day and the DI Nick Brown, were sitting on opposite sides of the double bed. Billy was in the bathroom on his job phone speaking in his soft Edinburgh accent, which was slightly amplified owing to the acoustics of the enclosed space. Dom was settling into the armchair by the window as Nick handed him his PNB and exhibit bags for his tape and the buff folder. Graham and Nick took the folder from him and began to work their way through the pages and photographs.

Graham addressed the whole room. "This is mint. It's like an offender's profile, you couldn't ask for anything else. Are we sure O'Toole has not been in the job? It's textbook stuff."

"Boss, this guy is fucking evil. It was like sitting at a table with Jekyll and Hyde. He's one of the spookiest men I've ever come across and that's saying something. O'Toole has it in him to kill this guy without help. He's hell bent on having this man killed. I've given him a two-to-four-week window, but I suggest we move as fast as we can on this," Dom said.

Graham replied, "The more I hear about O'Toole the more I agree with you, Dom."

Dom sealed the folder in an exhibit bag, knowing that Nick would open it once back at the nick to make photocopies, then place his original exhibit bag and the original folder in a new bag signed and sealed by him. Dom would have a copy of the folder in time for the next deployment. But for now, the team had work to do with the information contained in the typed pages and photographs.

Sam lifted her head from her magazine. "Do you want to sit here to do that, Dom?"

Tread carefully, Dom, Dom thought. *Is this an act of kindness and humanity from Sam, or is there another 'Sambush' on its way?* However, Dom said, "Yeah, that would be better, thanks, Sam, very gracious of you," trying not to sound suspicious.

Standing, and as she gathered her PNB and exhibit bags, Sam added, "This chair is giving me a numb bum and that armchair looks far more comfortable. Come on, swap ya."

Not kindness, pure self-comfort on her behalf, Dom thought. They exchanged positions and, to try to get the last word in Dom said, "Remember, Sam, that expensive magazine you're reading is an exhibit and needs bagging and tagging."

Still focused on the magazine, Sam said as she waved an exhibit bag in the air, "I know, I just want to finish this article about men who think they know everything, Dominic."

The rest of the room joined in on a moment of laughter. Dom shook his head and got on with the task in hand.

Once all the notes and exhibits, including the *Vogue* magazine, had been completed, they debriefed Graham while Nick made notes. Both men were delighted with the day's work and asked about Dom's availability over the coming week.

"No problem, boss, we have some slack in the office and other bits I got on are pretty flexible so feel free to use and abuse me," Dom said.

Graham smiled. "Thanks, Dom. Once again team, my thanks for turning up at short notice and doing such a professional job. I feel we've got a grip on this maniac. Thank you."

"Hear hear," chorused Nick and Billy.

A busy twenty-four hours for everyone involved, thought Dom. He also thought that Billy would be in bed fast asleep by eight o'clock, then had a second thought. *No, he won't, he'll be busy burning the midnight oil, again.*

That was the business done for the day and the three Operation Candle amigos went their separate ways. Sam jumped in the van with Phil and they headed down the road. Dom was feeling fatigued and was looking forward to a large whiskey on ice whilst watching something on Netflix. Perhaps he should have been looking forward to something or someone else, but he was too wrapped up in the job. Not so wrapped up that he had forgotten his boy's football match. Despite his troubles at home. He knew Judy would always encourage the father of her children to always be a big part in the kids' lives. Dom was grateful for that not that he needed any encouragement.

Chapter 43: Cops and Robbers

D om heard nothing from Billy for a couple of days, but he had other jobs on the go so that was fine as he knew if he needed him, he'd be on the phone, so Dom decided not to bother him.

Sam and Phil were looking forward to some time with their families at the end of the week. Sam planned to take her son to see a film and a rare visit to Mickey Ds. Phil was taking his wife and kids to see his mother. His kids loved Grandma. Under-cover officers have private lives and they always had reasons for their absences from the plot, the place of deployment. In the case of Operation Candle, Dom, Sam and Phil created the illusion they were busy successful businesspeople on the plot and had their fingers into a few lucrative pies. Those pies were fabricated business opportunities and served the purpose of covering for their absences.

Dom was looking forward to some down time. His lad was playing football again at the weekend, and he loved being there with the other parents, ranting and coaching from the touchline. The manager hated it when Dom turned up, but the other mums and dads loved it. He always had an answer or a one liner for the opposition adults. These dad activities were never affected by the relationship breakdown between Dom and Judy. Apart from sleeping in different bedrooms, things were as usual.

Judy was inquisitive about Dom's latest deployment as she sensed he was deep in thought. Dom told her it was a contract killing job and the guy was a real nutter. That was all. When his kids were young, they knew if Dad went into the dining room they had to stay out. That was where Dom had two phone lines on different regional numbers. The room was out of bounds. Those rules didn't change because his home life was changing.

Billy called Dom, asking him to attend an off-site meeting the next day and be ready to deploy if necessary. Dom arranged cover for Operation Candle and told Judy he wouldn't be back to look after the kids while she went out for dinner with her girlfriends. She'd have to arrange a babysitter, again. Judy shrugged it off because she knew his job was the third party in a strange ménage à trois. She knew Dom was no womaniser. In fact, she also knew he didn't have time nor the inclination to play the field. With a sigh and much resignation, she accepted the situation for what it was and no matter what she did, nothing would change.

Walking into Billy's office, Dom was given a brew and a copy of the buff folder to read and digest. The contents of the folder were amazingly detailed. Dom now completely understood Graham's comments at the first debrief when he wondered if O'Toole had ever been a copper. After reading the folder, Billy passed Dom a typed sheet of A4 which laid out a proposal covering the next meeting to the arrest phase. This had been drawn up between him and Graham. Dom was to call O'Toole today and arrange a meeting around five o'clock that evening in the car park of the same hotel where they had met previously.

"Tell him you need him to come with you to the gym car park and physically identify Terry out of the three men that jog to the gym. Once that's done and we are confident we have the right guy, things will move very quickly. Remind him to bring the twenty-five grand with him if he still wants to go through with the contract," Billy said.

"Then, two or three days later call him again and have a further meeting where you tell him you are ready to go. If asked, you are to tell him that Terry would be killed in what appeared to be a hit and run accident after he goes his separate way at the end of his jog home from the gym."

Graham had arranged photographs of what appeared to be an accident scene from his brother-in-law who worked in film and television. A stroke of genius by Graham, the pictures looked real. This was to back up the offer Dom would make if O'Toole wanted proof. Graham had also got the press office on board to make an appeal for witnesses to a serious accident on the road where the supposed accident would happen.

They were painting a picture for O'Toole to see and walk into.

Chapter 44: "Hello, Joe, is that you?"

Dom placed a new tape into a recording device before completing the usual introduction, then called O'Toole on the only number in the phone. That was the first time since O'Toole had been given the burner phone. O'Toole answered the phone after about three rings.

"Hello, Joe, is that you?"

"Yes, Harold, it's me. How are you?"

"Yes, I'm fine. How's things going your end?"

"Things are good and progressing nicely, Harold. I need to meet with you later today at the same hotel we met before at six o'clock this evening. Are you able to make that?"

"No worries. Six o'clock at the hotel."

"I'll meet you in the lounge as before, then we're going on to the gym so that you can give me a one hundred percent identification of Terry. Your file was brilliant, and I've found it very helpful in my work, but I want to make sure I get the right guy."

"Yes, of course. I'll be there at six."

"I'll see you this evening, Harold. Bye for now."

"Bye, Joe."

It was planned that the evening's events would be covered by surveillance of O'Toole's meeting with Dom, and Terry leaving the gym with his friends. The surveillance photograph would smudge the group of three and the team would describe all three men. Dom would have O'Toole describe Terry and what he was wearing to ensure that all descriptions and photographs matched Terry. This was to ensure they were all singing off the same hymn sheet. They? The undercover and surveillance teams.

O'Toole arrived at the hotel ten minutes early. Dom was sitting in his car and watched him arrive accompanied by a full surveillance team. Dom thought, *It's surreal watching it unfold in front of you. The team is good and blends into the environment naturally.*

Dom walked into the lounge and saw O'Toole sitting at the same table they occupied at the previous meeting. Dom clocked a couple of the surveillance team who looked just like ordinary customers sitting in the lounge. Dom's tape was running as he approached O'Toole. Then he explained to O'Toole they were going to the gym car park to wait for Terry and his mates to arrive. The photographs that he had supplied were good, but he wanted to be sure they got the right guy. O'Toole had no objection to the plan.

"Have you brought the money with you, Harold?"

"Yes, it's here." He tapped the satchel. "Would you like to check it?"

"Yes, please. Let's go to my car and we can have a bit of privacy. Once the money's right I'll drive us to the gym, and we can wait for Terry and his mates to arrive."

In the car, O'Toole produced twenty-five bundles of twenty-pound notes in one-thousand-pound bundles. Taking a Waitrose carrier bag from the door panel, Dom carefully thumbed each bundle ensuring that they each contained fifty notes. The notes were used and non-sequential. Dom put them into the Waitrose bag.Happy, Dom reached over and stuffed the bag under the front passenger seat.

Dom didn't want to make conversation with O'Toole. He let him chat away and Dom made appropriate noises to acknowledge he was listening but taking care not to ask any questions. Dom didn't want to get into talking in detail about the contract. There was now enough evidence to put a good case in front of a judge and jury. Dom knew it was now a case of closing off any escape routes he may try at trial or interview. They drove to the sports centre, with Dom parking the Merc near the entrance. The doorway was well illuminated, and identification was not a problem.

O'Toole broke the silence. "Here's the bastard. That's him in the yellow hi-visibility top and red leggings, wanker. Look at him, what a waste of space. Your days are numbered."

"Yeah, that's the guy I've been following. That's it, our work here is done."

Dom fired up the Mercedes and drove back to the hotel. On the way, Dom asked if he wanted proof that the contract had been fulfilled.

O'Toole looked confused. "What sort of proof? What do you mean?"

"Sometimes the contract holder wants the person to know where it has come from. I won't be able to do that because this is going to be a hit and run traffic accident. I can try to get a photograph if you want a souvenir. I imagine it will be on the local news."

"Yeah, a photograph of the bastard smashed up, dead on the side of the road would be a nice keepsake if you can get it."

"Okay. This time next week after he's been to the gym, and he leaves his mates on their jog home. He has about a mile along a lane alone. That's the spot. If he's not dead before, I'll make sure he's finished before I leave the scene and if possible, a photograph. I will ring you and we will meet up at the hotel. You will pay me the outstanding balance of twenty-five thousand pounds and hand me back the phone I gave you. I will hand you the photograph if I can get it. In the days after there will be stuff on the local radio, TV and the press on a serious hit and run accident and the police will be appealing for any witnesses. My advice to you is do not go and visit the scene. Stay away. The police will put a road check on looking for witnesses, people that use that lane or live in the area. The police will pull out all the stops out on this. Do not come to their attention. Once we shake hands and say goodbye to each other we will never see each other again. That's a lot of information there. Is everything clear, Harold?"

"Absolutely, Joe. I'm visiting my sister this week and therefore will not be at the dance class and there is no competition this weekend, so I won't be seeing him or Jean. I will await your call. Meet you here with the rest of the used notes and not sequential numbers, as previous. Photograph and return the phone. Clear as a bell, Joe."

"I'll say goodnight, Harold and look forward to seeing you next week."

Just as he was getting out, O'Toole turned to Dom. "Can I ask you what you are going to do with the car, are you going to drive here in it?"

"Don't you worry about the car, Harold. The car used for the job will be abandoned and torched some miles away from the scene. It will be on false plates and not traceable to me, you or anyone else. Hopefully the police will assume a hit and run by a couple of two bob crooks who panicked and drove off and torched the motor. The police can assume what they want, that doesn't concern me. It's where the evidence takes them and if we stick to the plan and the advice I've given you, it will take them nowhere near us."

"Okay, Joe. See you next week."

O'Toole got out and Dom drove off before he could get back to his car just in case O'Toole fancied doing a bit of a one-car follow on him. The more Dom got to know this evil bastard the more precautions he took.

Later, the usual debrief took place with the team, with the notes and exhibits all sorted, then Dom was off home, looking forward to some time with his kids. He also planned to start looking for somewhere to rent. He'd find some place close to Judy and the kids so he could continue being a good dad. He knew it was time too as it wasn't fair on Judy to have her estranged husband living permanently in the spare bedroom.

Chapter 45: Evil Bastard

One week later, Dom was back in the briefing location. Billy had moved the venue just to break the pattern and mix things up a bit. The plan was talked through and finalised. Once Dom had handed over the photograph and received the phone and money from O'Toole, he was to tell him to wait for ten minutes and then leave the hotel. It was planned for the arrest team to nick him at the table. DI Nick Brown handed Dom two polaroid photographs of a mangled and blood covered body lying by a hedgerow. The pictures looked real to Dom, and he was happy they would satisfy O'Toole. Dom put the photographs into a carrier bag which he folded around the photograph and stuck it in his jacket pocket.

That evening the surveillance team covered Terry at the gym and a second team was put on O'Toole to ensure he stuck to his usual routine. It was possible that O'Toole might go to the gym to take some sort of macabre satisfaction out of what was in store for Terry. Keeping Terry under surveillance was to ensure he kept to his gym visit just in case O'Toole had something in place to confirm Terry's attendance at the sports centre. The boss had to cover all bases. This was the pinnacle of the operation and there was no room for cutting corners or complacence.

Dom waited at the briefing location until he got updates from DS Paul Hindley that Terry was at the gym and the other team confirmed O'Toole was at home. Terry was seen to leave the gym, jogging together with his two mates. The surveillance team used some observation points, OPs, on the route used by the three joggers. Once they had gone through one OP, they would leapfrog ahead to the next one. Now, Dom learned Terry had departed company from his two mates and was jogging along the lane. He was alone and the lane was quiet. Dom had about a twenty-minute drive to the hotel where he was due to meet up with O'Toole but built in an extra ten minutes for the trip. He added a further twenty minutes to the half hour to allow for the 'killing,' taking the photo then torching the car. He couldn't help clock-watching for the next twenty minutes until he called O'Toole.

"Hi, it's me. Are you available for a meeting at the hotel, Harold? Make sure you bring that paperwork we agreed with you."

"Yes, of course. I'll see you there in about half an hour."

Dom didn't need further conversation, so he hung up. He wanted to get there before O'Toole and drove to the hotel steadily, keeping within the speed limits. On entering the lounge, Dom had achieved his goal. No sign of O'Toole. He took up position at the table where he could see anyone entering the lounge and approaching him. After five minutes, O'Toole came through the automatic doors and walked towards Dom. Within seconds of O'Toole entering, a man and a woman followed him. Dom betted with himself they were members of the surveillance team. O'Toole had his satchel slung over his shoulder in his usual style. Dom and O'Toole greeted each other with a handshake and sat down. As they did so, two men followed by a third man entered the hotel. The arrest team were now with him.

"Harold, for obvious reasons I don't want to hang around too long. Have you got the money and the phone?"

He tapped his satchel and nodded. "Everything go well, Joe?"

"Better than I expected. I don't think he heard me coming I was able to hit him fast and dead centre. He flew like a pigeon over the roof. I must have been doing sixty when I hit him, fucking hell of a noise. I left long skid marks after the impact and reversed back. He was a fucking mess. His legs were pointing in all directions. His back was broken, he was bent in two, the back of his head almost touching his backside. You would not recognise him. There was shit and blood everywhere. I got a couple of snaps for you at no additional cost. Happy?"

This evil bastard stopped short of asking Dom to repeat the description. He reached into his satchel and produced two large brown envelopes and placed them on the table. Dom picked them up and looking into both, he saw rolls of twenty-pound notes.

Dom looked up at him. "I think I can trust it's all there, Harold. Have you got the phone?"

Reaching once more into the satchel, O'Toole retrieved the mobile phone and placed it on the table next to the brown envelopes. As he did so, Dom took the folded-up carrier bag out of his pocket and pushed it across the table towards O'Toole, then invited him to have a quick look.

Dom smiled as he said, "You might like what's in there. Don't have nightmares."

Without taking the photographs out, O'Toole looked into the bag and smiled. "He's dead, then?"

"Very dead."

"Thank you, Joe, you have done me a great service."

As Dom rose from his seat he collected the envelopes and the phone, then held out his hand.

O'Toole got to his feet and shook Dom's hand.

"Goodbye, Harold," Dom said.

Dom heard the farewell repeated as he turned and walked away. Once outside the automatic doors, he looked back at O'Toole who was now in the company of three men and a woman. One of the men was placing handcuffs on O'Toole as another picked up the carrier bag and satchel.

Dom took a few seconds to reflect and thought, *Good job, Dom. That's one evil bastard who will be doing a lot of jail time.*

The next day it was life as normal, whatever that is. Sam and Phil were busy looking busy without being busy. That was a deliberate ploy. They had fostered some new relationships with people of interest to the operational team on Operation Candle. Now separated and renting his robber's hideout, Dom's wife had given him strict instructions to be at the school for their daughter's parents' evening. He wouldn't miss that for anything or anyone. He also had to make some arrangements to progress the Spanish lorry job currently on the back burner. Dom had just finished doing that when his job phone rang. Answering, he heard Sam's voice, "Fancy a quick drink, Dom?"

"Another time, Sam. I'm off to my daughter's parents' evening soon."

"Okay, no problem. Another time, then."

The rest is history as they say.

Chapter 46: Jack Tar

The Jack Tar story started with Sam's cover officer, John Williams, better known as JW to the people he worked with, calling Sam on her job phone only twenty-four hours before the trade involving fifty-thousand quid's worth of ecstasy pills and a bent prison officer. What else do you need to know?

The trade, or purchase of drugs, was planned for two o'clock in the afternoon at Bedford railway station, and like a good ex-military man 'Jack Tar,' the target, walked in with a rucksack slung over one shoulder at five to. He was dressed in a tracksuit which showed off his powerful frame. *Yeah, this guy would look at home in a gym*, Sam thought, as she also saw Mon ogling the target. Mon was her fellow undercover officer. Jack was only about five six or seven but had broad shoulders that tapered to a thin waistline. Sam knew beforehand she was potentially just about to have a row with this meathead over a change in plan. Stop and think how you would feel. *This guy's a drug dealer and a corrupt prison officer, how will he react when told there's to be a change of plan?*

Maybe, just like you, Sam was not looking forward to the possible confrontation, but knew she had to tell him about the change in a firm, confident and controlling manner and keep the job alive. Months of hard work by so many officers now rested on her shoulders. *A lot of responsibility for a Detective Constable*, she thought as Jolly Jack nodded in acknowledgment at the two women, then walked towards Mon and Sam who were sitting at a table. He joined them and they made their introductions. It's not like walking into a business meeting when you shake hands and introduce yourself by name and position within the company. The intros went like this. "Hi Jack, I'm Sam and this is Mon."

He flicked his eyes towards Mon and then back to Sam. "Hi, everything cool with you two ladies? You got the money with you?"

Sam gave him a reassuring smile. "Yeah, it's close by, darling, I just need to test a couple of the little fellas. No offence, Jack, but that's how we do things. You're okay with that?" She was referring to the pills as 'little fellas.'

He nodded. "Let's go. My car's outside, you can crack a couple while I drive you round the block."

Here we go, Sam thought. "Here's the thing, Jack. I would rather we did the whole deal here, sweetie. We will come out to your car. Mon will take three pills from the parcel and test them in the ladies' loo. You and I will come back here while Mon is doing her stuff. If they come up to scratch, we'll do the trade boot to boot in the car park. How's that with you, Jack, sweetie?" She focussed on his face in the hope of seeing a positive reaction to the new plan. You must know that feeling like time stopped. *Shit, he's not happy*, she thought.

"What's the issue, ladies, you think I might kidnap you and rip you off?"

Sam smiled, saying, "No, darling, I just like to keep things simple. Mon can do her stuff quickly in the loo rather than in the back of a car, fewer moving parts. We can have this over in a couple of minutes and be on our merry way. What do you say?"

He hesitated for a few seconds. "Okay, all the same to me, ladies. Yeah, let's do that."

Sam stood and said, "Shall we go then and get this show on the road?" Mon also got up from her seat.

Jack stayed sitting. "No need to go out to the car park, I've got them here in my rucksack, ladies."

Tosser, Sam thought, *amateur. You never walk into a trade with the parcel.* Her confidence was boosted as she and Mon sat down again.

"Where's the money?" he asked.

"It's in the back of my car, do you want to see it?" Sam said.

He shook his head. "No, you test the merchandise and if you are happy, we will go out to the car and we'll get on with it." He pushed the rucksack towards Mon with his foot and invited Mon to help herself. She reached into the rucksack with a small pair of nail tweezers. After a few seconds she pulled out three small pills. Taking her shoulder bag with her, she told Sam and Jolly Jack she'd be back in a couple of minutes and walked off towards the ladies.

"How do you know Dave, then?" asked Jack.

Sam recognised the name as the undercover officer who had been deployed on the job before her and Mon. "He works for my fella. He can be a bit Marmite, if you know what I mean." She didn't want to talk about Dave in case he'd mentioned something to Jack that she was unaware of. *Fall back on your training, experience, and trade craft, Sam*, she thought. "I know his girlfriend better than him. Do you know her, Janet?"

He again shook his head. "No, it surprises me that someone

213

would want to spend time with him." They both laughed. Sam continued to talk about the fictional Janet, basing the conversation on a good friend of hers, so it was easy to fill the time with lies that were close to the truth. You may agree, it's easier to remember the lie by keeping close to the truth.

Mon returned after a few minutes. Jack seemed pleased to see her as Sam had blathered on about the imaginary Janet.

"All good, Sam," Mon said as she reached the table.

"Excellent, hon, good job," Sam said and again got to her feet and said with enthusiasm, "Should we?" With nothing more said they walked out of the buffet towards the Toyota four by four. Jack kept hold of his rucksack. Sam had her handbag over her shoulder. As they walked out of the station building and into the open space of the car park, Sam removed the bag from her shoulder and placed it under her left arm. *The signal.*

Within seconds the silence of the car park was shattered with shouts of, "Police, police. Get down. Keep your hands away from your body. Get down get on the ground, hands out."

Sam had been nicked a few times on the plot, and perhaps you can guess it can sometimes be too realistic. This wasn't too bad. Not so for Jolly Jack, he was marched off, cuffed behind and guided into the back of a plain police car. As it drove off, Sam saw him watching Mon and her being handcuffed and placed into different plain vehicles.

It had been exactly twenty-four hours since her cover officer had phoned her. Dom had been snoring on the sofa. James had been fighting whoever on his PS2 and she had been struggling to arrange childcare. Since then, she had a full on twenty-four hours that ended up with her in handcuffs, signing for fifty-thousand pounds as buy money and recovering enough pills to choke a donkey. After Sam had completed her notes and exhibits, she jumped into her BMW and set off back to Bedbug, Mum and maybe Dom. *What's he been doing over the last twenty-four hours? Let's have a bit of Frankie Valli on the sounds.*

That was the last time Sam saw Jolly Jack for almost a year.

Chapter 47: Twenty-Four Hours Earlier

Sam loves Dom, but sometimes he could really tick her off. They say opposites attract but Sam knew she and Dom were both alphas. Sam reckoned it added spice to their relationship. They both knew having the same job was a help rather than a hindrance. Theirs was a candid relationship and one that didn't blossom for some time. At first, Sam thought Dom was full of himself. In time, as she saw more of him in their undercover life, Sam started to see a softer side to him. They were both aware of each other's baggage in that Dom was on the way to a second divorce and Sam was long divorced from James' father, Ken.

Sam and Dom hadn't yet committed to living together permanently. They were at a stage where Dom would occasionally stay over at Sam's home, sleeping in the spare room and doing the school run if she had to get away on the hurry up. They had just finished Sunday lunch and a bottle or two of wine and Dom asked if it was okay to sleep in the spare room as he had an early start and needed to be away by seven for a briefing at ten o'clock. Sam told him that would be fine, and Dom promptly fell asleep on the sofa. Within a few minutes, Sam heard Dom's light snoring. Looking over at the sofa, she saw he was face down, sleeping soundly and completely flat out. The next thing

Sam heard was the ring tone of her job phone. Answering, she heard a familiar voice. "Hi Sam, it's me, are you all right to talk?" No introduction needed – it was John Williams, aka JW, from the cover office.

"Hi John, yeah, that noise you can hear in the background isn't GCHQ listeners. It's Dom snoring. What are you after, hon?"

John chuckled and asked Sam to give Dom his best regards when he came out of his coma. "Sam, a force in the midlands needs your expertise. They have a job that's been running for some time and the opposition have called the day of the trade on for tomorrow without notice."

Sam asked the obvious question. "Why?" There is always a reason 'why' we or the opposition change the plan at short notice. It may be a red light, stop and think. It may be an amber light, let's think about this and how we go forward safely. It might be a green light, something or nothing, but the question needed to be asked.

"Why?" John continued, "It's a drug's buy of ecstasy, a lot of the little fellas, a lot of Es. Fifty thousand pounds worth. I'm talking to the cover officer from their area and the info is still coming in and I don't have the full picture yet. I'm in the process of pulling things together. I need you at a briefing in a hotel at Luton Airport at eleven o'clock tomorrow, but before that I need to meet up with you at Toddington Services on the M1 motorway by nine o'clock, when I'll have more info to bring you up to speed before the main briefing, and sort out how you and we are going to do the trade."

Sam's first thought was James, the school run and arranging overnight childcare. She was not going to give John a sniff of her difficulties in meeting his timetable. "Toddington at nine, sweetie, see you there, milky coffee for me." No indication from her of how she was going to make that happen.

"One more thing before you go. You'll need someone to work with to test the gear. Any thoughts?" John said.

Yeah, loads of thoughts, John, but not on the National Index unless we have someone with a skill base in school runs and childcare. Keeping her thoughts unspoken, Sam said, "What about that geeky looking guy I worked with in Liverpool? He used the name Tim; he was good around the gear." Tim was young looking for a thirty-year-old, slight frame, glasses, pale complexion. He'd been a street buyer of heroin, cocaine, and ecstasy, a Test Purchase Officer, (TPO), before taking the step up to a level one UCO.

"Okay, I'll get busy on the phones. Thanks, Sam, I knew I could count on you. Great way to spend a Sunday afternoon. I'm going up there later today to sort out as much as I can before you arrive. See you at Toddington."

Yeah, great way to spend the afternoon. "No worries, darling, see you tomorrow."

As Sam put the phone down Dom piped up, "That sounded interesting." It was only his voice as he hadn't opened his eyes or moved. He knew Sam would share with him what she could, and right now she was going to share her problem rather than any details about the job. James had disappeared upstairs an hour ago and she could hear explosions and machine guns coming from his bedroom which only meant one thing: he was fighting a battle with his mates online.

Sam now had her own battle to fight. "I've got to be away super early in the morning, babe. Can you cover the school run?"

"Nope, babe, I'm in the same situation—got to be away

early." He still had his eyes shut and hadn't moved an inch. His tone was matter of fact. Sam knew the location and time of his briefing and knew he could do the school run and get there in time if the wind was blowing in the right direction and the traffic was kind. But he hated being late. *Thanks for your support, Dom*, she thought. She was being sarcastic but because she cared for him, any extra words remained unspoken. *On to plan 'B,'* Sam thought.

"Hi, Mum, how's things? What you up to?" Mum half expected what was coming next as Sam had spoken to her on the phone earlier, so a follow up call could only mean one thing. "I've just had a phone call from work, and I've got a really early start in the morning. Any chance you and Dad could do the school drop off and pick up for me tomorrow? Dom's here, but he's got to be away early too." Sam knew her mum was a brick. Without her support and her dad's, those who doubted her ability, drive and desire to work undercover as a single mum may have been proved right. She was not going to give some governor – a line manager – sat behind a desk the satisfaction. "Thanks, Mum, love you, see you later." As she put the phone down, she gave Dom a playful dig in the ribs. "You awake?"

He opened one eye and squeezed the other eye tight shut. "Um, what does I'll see you later mean?" Lowering her head to his squinty eye, Sam gently gave him a peck on his lips. "It means you are definitely in the spare room as agreed, because Mum's coming over later and staying over to do the school run."

"I'll be away extra early in the morning then," he muttered.

"Oh, don't sulk, babe, you had first refusal."

Chapter 48: Legend Car

C hildcare issue sorted, Sam made for her 'go bag' in case it turned into an overnighter. That bag contained sufficient clothing and toiletries to survive in the field for a couple of days. The red Adidas sports holdall contained her gym stuff and swim kit. It too was always ready to go alongside the 'go bag.' Her covert handbag was in a hide upstairs. The bag itself wasn't covert. The contents were. They confirmed her alias – part of her legend as it's known in covert operations.

James didn't know where the hide was when he was younger, but as he grew and understood more, Sam believed he had worked it out for himself without saying a word to her. After Dom moved in, he also knew as he used it for his own tricky stuff on the odd occasion. She had known UCOs who had their house screwed, broken into, by opportunist thieves. Their hide was the first thing they checked on discovering the burglary to make sure whatever they put in there was still intact. Satisfied it was, they would breathe a sigh of relief, then manage the burglary as the rest of us would.

Sam's car, a silver BMW M3, was fully loaded with all the buttons and bells, fuelled and ready to go. This was her legend car registered to her in her pseudonym, Samantha Smith, at a covert address. The car suited her deep, long-term legend of a successful entrepreneurial businesswoman, selling lingerie, sportswear, designer handbags and clothing. She wouldn't need to promenade any of her legend at tomorrow's gig, a quick in and out job. They were there to do the trade, not exchange CVs.

She bumped into Dom as he appeared on the landing coming out of the bathroom. Whispering and with a cheeky grin, she said, "Morning, darling, how did you sleep?" Sam quickly kissed his freshly shaved face. Before they made their way downstairs, she quietly popped into James' bedroom to give him a soft, gentle kiss on his forehead without disturbing him. "Love you, Bedbug. Mummy will be home soon."

Passing her mum's bedroom and just as she started down the stairs, Sam heard her quietly say, "Be careful, lass, don't worry about anything back here."

"Okay, Mum, go back to sleep. Love you, and thanks." Dom gave her a hand putting her bags into the boot of the Beemer. Before climbing into the driving seat, they had a cuddle and kiss in the garage. They both wished each other luck and stressed the importance of staying safe.

"Don't take any chances, you lunatic," he said.

"Ditto, you big lump," Sam replied as she pulled out of the garage. It was four thirty in the morning and she had a long drive ahead of her. *Let's have a bit of Frankie Valli on the sounds system.*

Chapter 49: Monica

Sam called JW about fifteen minutes away from Toddington Services. It went straight to voice mail. She left a message to say she would be there in fifteen minutes. On arriving at the services, she was in desperate need of a pee. After a trip to the loo, she walked into the food area and had a look around for JW. Sam clocked him in a corner of the eating area – exactly where she would have sat, with a full view of the area. He was with a female she didn't recognise.

Sam was introduced to Monica who asked to be called Mon, who had a similar background to Tim so knew her stuff and had been deployed on other jobs. She was in her thirties, with short, straight blonde hair and very lean. In Sam's opinion she didn't look like she was a stranger to recreational drugs. *Ideal*.

JW said, "The opposition don't want to deal with blokes. Apparently, they didn't like Dave, the previous UCO, telling them how the deal would go down and didn't want him anywhere near the trade. He's salvaged the operation in a phone call and agreed to send two girls. They were happy. That's the first problem I think we have boxed off. The other thing I've been told is that their guy on the pavement is a serving prison officer in Bedford Jail. He's been recruited by an inmate to do their dealing on the outside while they are doing ten years on the inside. They call their man 'Jack Tar' because he was a PTI... a Physical Training Instructor in the Royal Navy."

"Bloody hell, JW, this is going to be entertaining. I'm already head fucked with everything I've heard. What's your thoughts, Mon?" Sam said.

Mon looked relaxed and said, "Yeah, whatever you think will work, Sam."

What sort of answer is that? Mon gave me the impression she was on the gear. I think I will be the lead on this job, Sam thought.

JW and Sam came up with a strategy and game plan that JW would run out to the operational team prior to them joining the briefing. That was JW's job, politics, as Sam called it. At the briefing it was agreed that the trade would take place at Bedford train station. Sam and Mon were to put the fifty thousand pounds in a safe deposit locker at the station, then meet 'Jack Tar' in the buffet bar on the main platform as already arranged. Then Sam was to change the plan again. She had to convince him that her tester of the gear, Mon, would test the pills in the ladies' toilet instead of in the back of his car as he drove them around Bedford. That shit tactic was crap and dangerous, not to mention difficult to control for the operational team. It could leave Sam and Mon at risk of a rip off and harm. The fifty thousand belonged to the police. Some would say the taxpayer. Whatever, it needed looking after. That's why they had an armed response within the surveillance and arrest team. Please don't think they put covert armed cops on the pavement to protect the UCOs. It's all about the money, Sam would tell you.

Mon and Sam counted out the fifty thousand pounds and Sam signed for it. They then bundled it up in rolls of one thousand pounds. Each bundle was held together with an elastic band

and the lot was put into an orange Sainsbury carrier bag which Sam put into a pull along suitcase. The signal for the arrest team to move in and effect the arrest was agreed. Sam would take her handbag from her shoulder and place it in under her left arm. On seeing this the arrest team would strike and arrest all three of them.

With fifty grand in the suitcase and the use of one of their covert vehicles, a Toyota four by four, they set off for Bedford train Station.

On arrival at the station Mon and Sam parked up directly outside the station entrance. Sam estimated they were no more than fifty feet to the main entrance. Sam took the case containing the money and walked into the station. The lockers were all shut and locked with no keys in the locks. Sam approached the ticket office and asked the guy behind the glass how she could get a left luggage locker.

His reply in a strong Yorkshire accent made her smile. "Sorry, me duck, the lockers are out of action as directed by the local bobbies because of bomb threats."

Sam thought, *Would that be the same 'bobbies' who have just briefed me?* This was a case of adapt, improvise, and overcome.

Mon looked like a prematurely ageing rocker which was ideal for her job on that day. She asked Sam, "What we are going to do with the money?" Sam thought for a moment. She didn't have time to make a phone call and ask for a decision. She had to work this out for herself, taking all the moving parts of the operation into consideration; the surveillance and arrest teams, the armed team, safe control of the fifty thousand pounds and control the exchange with Jolly Jack in a location that worked for everyone. She had to think and act fast. *How can I keep control of the money and still get the ecstasy and the dealer?* Sam thought, until she said, "Right, this is what we're going to do. We'll stick it in the back of the four by four."

Mon thought for a moment then said, "Do you think it will be safe there, Sam?"

Sam laughed and replied, "You watch where the armed surveillance goes when we put the dosh in the back."

As the two undercover officers walked back into the station after depositing the fifty thousand in the back of the Toyota, they made for the buffet bar on the main platform and noticed they were unescorted. The armed surveillance had stayed with the money. They still had an arrest team and members of the surveillance team with them. Sam called JW using cryptic words in case anyone overheard her. "I've had to leave my suitcase in the back of the car, darling, the lockers are out of service."

He cottoned on and confirmed he understood when he said, "Is that the case containing the paperwork?"

"Yeah, spot on darling, must go, love you, bye," Sam said.

JW replied, "Love you too."

You think sorting out childcare is stressful, try doing this for a job at the same time, Sam thought.

Mon and Sam settled into the buffet. Sam went to the ladies to switch on her recording device and made the normal introduction first. Like a speaking clock, she announced the time and date followed by, "I am a serving police officer in the United Kingdom and for the purpose of this operation I wish to be known as Sam. I am at Bedford train station in the company of a female I know as Mon. We are waiting for a man by the name of Jack Tar who is looking to sell us fifty thousand pounds worth of ecstasy tablets. I will leave this recording device running until it is safe to switch it off." Sam then returned to the buffet and Mon went to the ladies and carried out the same procedure.

Once Mon came back to the table, they only spoke to confirm the time or order a drink of tea or coffee. There was no small talk or banter. Everything they captured on the recording was evidence and could end up being played in Luton Crown Court in months to come. You already know what happened after Jack Tar showed up.

Chapter 50: Crown Court Warning

After much more water had passed under Sam's undercover bridge, she received notice to appear at Luton Crown Court in the case of R v Jolly Jack. He was pleading not guilty. Why? What defence is he running? He's bang to rights.

Mon had received the same warning. JW and Mon's cover officer made all the arrangements for their entrance into the court building, avoiding the public and public areas. They sat in a private room in the court building reserved for the judge and court staff. They had been given copies of their statements to refresh memories, their pocket notebooks and the transcript of the covert recording. Mon didn't have one of those from her device because it didn't work on the day. Operator error or the device just went tech, it happens. It was in their favour Sam was with Jolly Jack all the time and had a contemporaneous record of all conversations.

Sam was called to give evidence and entered the court room from a side door. The last time dear old Jolly Jack saw her she wore her blonde hair long and loose on her shoulders, her face fully made up. She wore killer heels and had long painted fingernails, a look Sam was very comfortable with and went with her legend. Not today. She was Detective

Constable Samantha Smith. Her hair up in a chignon pleat, light makeup, court shoes and navy suit. Professional police officer. The witness box was screened off from the public and press. Jolly Jack and his defence team could see her as could the prosecution barrister and the CPS team. The clerk of the court, the jury and the judge could also see her. Sam took the oath and followed up with, "I am a serving police officer in the United Kingdom and for the purpose of this operation I was known as Sam and with leave of the court I ask permission to give my evidence in that name. I do have my police warrant card with me should you wish to see it, your Honour."

Jolly Jack got seven years.

Sam had a long drive home listening to Frankie Valli and thinking, *I've got the best job in the world.*

Her thoughts also wandered to Operation Candle, her son James, Dom, the new man in her life then she felt a surge of happiness pulse through her very being.

Afterword

Do you wonder what Operation Candle was all about? 'Undercover Legends' is planned as a series featuring not only Dom and Sam but other undercover officers as well as some villains of the piece. The next book in the series will be *Operation Candle* and it will be on pre-order soon at a discounted launch price.

It was a unique undercover operation set up to counter an intelligence black hole in a fictional town. Dom, Sam and Phil devised a plan to embed themselves in the community with Sam posing as a businesswoman operating an online lingerie, designer handbags and clothing business. Phil's cover story was an online business selling sports gear. With the help of a police technical support department, they got to work building websites, arranging covert personal and business bank accounts, credit cards, driving licences and passports.

At the outset, Dom said to Phil and Sam, "You never know, there could be some airmiles in this job."

Little did he know, he was right. Operation Candle was an amazing 'bit of work.'

Any undercover officer has a front and backstage existence, a bit like an actor. The front is on the stage performing a role. Backstage is partly his or her private life and in part the support and backup from the cover officers and the team. Those parts are the life support system enabling the actors' performances. You can find out more about the backstage existence of Dom and Sam by downloading a free eBook *Meet Mr and Mrs Smith*. It will help the reader understand what makes them tick. To download your free copy, go to davidlecourageux.com

Please consider leaving a review of this book, *Undercover Legends*. Just a few sentences will do, and they mean such a lot to writers. Thank you!

About the Author

David Le Courageux is the pen name for the writing team of Dominic Smith and Stephen Bentley. The only real name out of those three is Stephen Bentley. Just like Mr and Mrs Smith, he too is a former undercover police officer.

Mr and Mrs Smith were the stars of CrimeCon 2021 held in London where they made a personal appearance on a blacked-out stage to preserve their anonymity. CrimeCon is billed as the world's largest true crime event and is now held annually in both the United States and the United Kingdom. Dominic and Samantha were billed as the Real Mr and Mrs Smith – Undercover Legends. Following that event, the media showed a lot of interest in the Mr and Mrs Smith stories. The inquiries came from print and online publications and the film and TV industry. Talks are ongoing about the Mr and Mrs Smith franchise.

Stephen Bentley was also a barrister in London practising criminal law for fourteen years. Since retirement, he has written fifteen books including his best-selling Operation Julie memoir, originally independently published but the UK & Commonwealth rights have now been acquired by Penguin Random House UK. An 8-part TV series based on that book is in development. Stephen also co-wrote *Operation George: A Gripping True Crime Story of an Audacious Undercover Sting* with Mark Dickens, a pseudonym and another former undercover police officer.

His crime fiction includes the Steve Regan Undercover Cop Thrillers and the Detective Matt Deal Thrillers. He is a member of the Crime Writers' Association, the Society of Authors, and the Alliance of Independent Authors.

You can connect with me on:

🌐 https://davidlecourageux.com

📘 https://www.facebook.com/undercoverlegends

Also by David Le Courageux

BOOKS ABOUT UNDERCOVER POLICE OFFICERS BY DAVID LE COURAGEUX AND STEPHEN BENTLEY

COMING SOON

Operation Candle, Book 2 Undercover Legends by David Le Courageux

NONFICTION

Undercover: Operation Julie – The Inside Story by Stephen Bentley at https://books2read.com/u/b627eJ

Operation George: A Gripping True Crime Story of an Audacious Undercover Sting by Mark Dickens and Stephen Bentley at https://books2read.com/b/OPERATIONGEORGE

FICTION

The Steve Regan Undercover Cop Thrillers Trilogy by Stephen Bentley at https://books2read.com/b/meeyRZ

The Secret: A Prequel to the Gripping Steve Regan Undercover Cop Thrillers by Stephen Bentley at https://books2read.com/b/mvZ7xq

BONUS MATERIAL: OPERATION GEORGE EXCERPTS
The Targets

The following true story is not about Rosemary Nelson, the

Troubles *per se* nor Northern Ireland, although they feature out of necessity. We feel that from the outset it is worthwhile to set out a background to the events and locations of this book and a brief history of the Troubles in that part of Northern Ireland. Whilst this book tells the amazing story of possibly the most audacious undercover sting in the world, we also acknowledge the grief suffered by so many on both sides of the sectarian divide in that part of the United Kingdom. In writing this book, we can assure you we also felt the pain endured by so many innocent people.

William James Fulton and Muriel Gibson were from Portadown, a small town in County Armagh, Northern Ireland. Sadly, it is better known as the scene of the Drumcree conflict rather than the birthplace of notable people like Lady Mary Peters (Olympic athlete), Gloria Hunniford (TV personality) and Martin O' Neill (football manager). It is located about twenty-five miles southwest of Belfast. In the 1980s and 1990s its population was made up of about seventy percent Protestants and almost thirty percent Catholics. Garvaghy Road is in the middle of an area of housing that is largely populated by Catholics. Lurgan is a short drive away; about six miles separates it from Portadown. Lurgan was the location of Rosemary Nelson's law practice.

The Drumcree conflict is a dispute over the right of Protestants and loyalists to hold parades mainly to commemorate the so-called Glorious Revolution of 1688. The occasion is known by many as 'The Twelfth.' It was first held in the late 18th century in Ulster and it celebrates the victory of Protestant King William of Orange over Catholic King James II at the Battle of the Boyne in 1690, which began the Protestant Ascendancy in Ireland. Residents of Garvaghy Road and the surrounding

Catholic district object to what they view as "triumphalist" Orange marches through their area. Rosemary Nelson, a Catholic solicitor, was the figurehead and spokesperson for the Garvaghy Road Residents' Coalition as well as representing the coalition in legal matters until she was assassinated on 15 March 1999. Sam Kinkaid, the RUC officer who played a leading role in the investigation of Rosemary Nelson's murder, described the area (Portadown) as "second only to North Belfast in terms of sectarianism.[1]"

The sophisticated bomb device that blew up Rosemary Nelson's car and killed her is where our story begins. A loyalist paramilitary splinter group naming themselves the Red Hand Defenders claimed responsibility for the killing. At that time, William James Fulton and Muriel Landry née Gibson (referred to as Gibson throughout the remainder of this book) were members of the Loyalist Volunteer Force – the LVF. Soon after the bombing, Fulton fled to the United States and Gibson relocated to England.

In this story of Operation George, all the names of the undercover police officers (UCOs) used are pseudonyms. Some are the same aliases as used in evidential transcripts and sanctioned by the judge to preserve their anonymity whilst giving evidence at the trials of William James Fulton and Muriel Gibson at Belfast Crown Court. The names or nicknames of other UCOs and Cover Officers are fabricated aliases to protect their anonymity and thus prevent any kind of criminal retribution against them or their families. In the same vein, the authors are sparing in using details of any undercover officer such as physical descriptions, accents, backgrounds, and the like to preserve anonymity.

When Julie Met George

Operation Julie and Operation George are light years away from each other in more ways than one. Undercover policing has drastically changed owing to modern 'UK Police PLC' attitudes and policies. The contrasts between 1970s Operation Julie and 21st Century Operation George undercover policing are like night and day.

Perhaps now is an opportune moment to explain what is entailed to become a Level 1 UCO then to be entered into the national register. It's a world apart from the Operation Julie days when straight from being a member of a surveillance team, a detective would be asked by a boss if they wanted to go undercover. No training in those days. They made up a back story on the fly and then they were straight into the deep end. Sink or swim!

For some time now, undercover officers are recruited and must attend a national training course. They are evaluated to see if they are suitable and are eventually set free to establish a legend and back story. Those are the two things they will fall back on and carry with them for the remainder of their undercover careers. Essentially, it's a case of who they say they are and not who they really are. They will spend time in certain locations, establishing their faces by socialising and getting to be known in the area as Mr X or Mrs Y. That strengthens their credentials if someone checks them out. Occasionally, they may have to repeat that exercise if there is a good reason to change location. If an UCO has special skills, so much the better. For example, Robbie, one of the Operation George UCOs, appeared to have a licence to drive trucks, as it's known from the transcripts that he held himself out as a lorry driver in his dealings with Jim Fulton.

Unlike Bentley's pioneering undercover days, as described in his memoir Operation Julie, these Operation George officers belong to a modern era of covert policing. The story of Operation George highlights the sophisticated methods deployed by modern law enforcement. Those methods and techniques are all Bentley hoped and wished for when he wrote the chapter 'The Future of Undercover Policing' in his memoir. Indeed, they go beyond that and demonstrate the changes in policing attitudes and a resolute commitment to engage in proactive intelligence-led policing to combat organised crime and terrorism.

We need to add that even in Seventies undercover work, the targets of investigations were aware of undercover methods. As time passes, covert operations step up, invent new tactics, use the latest technology, all to keep one step ahead of the smartest criminal enterprise. The future may involve the use of drones, negating the need for human covert policing. It is not far-fetched to suggest that criminal activities, including meetings when crimes are planned, may soon be recorded both in audio and video. It is not hard to imagine with the arrival of 'smart cities', as referenced by the head of the UK intelligence agency, GCHQ. No wonder many criminals are paranoid. Even now, they will challenge innocents in a belief they may be undercover officers (UCOs). In fact, Jim Fulton did just that when telling the Operation George detectives he thought some of his neighbours in Cornwall were MI5 undercover people.

He was wrong. The "undercover people" were surrounding him, socialising with him, working with him, paying him as an employee, talking to him daily for the best part of two years. During that time, he was recorded on audio tapes, the 'product' of which eventually became the damning evidence sending him to jail with no prospect of release for twenty-five years.

Genocide

Over fifty thousand hours of conversations between William James Fulton and undercover officers engaged on Operation George were secretly recorded. In one of those recordings, Fulton said, "… They've got to shoot a Catholic once a week … about once a week and that's why they broke away. That's why the LVF broke away from the UVF was because they weren't killing enough Catholics. And the LVF wanted a Catholic per week killing."

Put yourself in the shoes of that undercover officer – how would you react to such disturbing words? These undercover officers are to be admired as the consummate professionals they truly are. They don't flinch, berate, judge or ask questions. Instead, they associate, infiltrate, befriend their target, and covertly gather the evidence for a future day of reckoning.

On the 11th of March 2021, a BBC World News article reported that, "The term genocide was coined in 1943 by the Jewish-Polish lawyer Raphael Lemkin, who combined the Greek word 'genos' (race or tribe) with the Latin word 'cide' (to kill). After witnessing the horrors of the Holocaust, in which every member of his family except his brother was killed, Dr Lemkin campaigned to have genocide recognised as a crime under international law.

His efforts gave way to the adoption of the United Nations Genocide Convention in December 1948, which came into effect in January 1951. Article Two of the convention defines genocide as 'any of the following acts committed with the intent to destroy, in whole or in part, a national, ethnic, racial or *religious* [our emphasis] group ...'"

This Operation George story has genocide at its centre. It's also the remarkable story of a brave, experienced, elite group of undercover officers and their forward-thinking boss, who conceptualised then executed a most brilliant plan to bring a terrorist to justice.

Interview Room, Belfast

On 12 June 2001, Constable Pierce of the Devon and Cornwall Constabulary, together with a specialist armed arrest team, arrested Jim Fulton at his Plymouth home under the Prevention of Terrorism Act. To Fulton's surprise, he was flown to Belfast under armed guard in a military helicopter. His surprise turned to fear as he started to cry like a baby, dreading that he was about to be assassinated and thrown into the dark waters of the Irish Sea.

By the time he had been processed at a Belfast holding centre, Fulton had reverted to type: a cocksure individual who thought he had nothing to worry about. That overconfidence was on display at the earliest stages of the disclosure interviews. Those interviews are mandatory under the umbrella of the Police and Criminal Evidence Act (PACE) and were conducted in the presence of a well-known Belfast solicitor.

Fulton was settling into a chair in the stark interview room, listening closely to the introductory disclosure material articulated by an interviewing officer, undoubtedly thinking, *I'll be out of here soon.*

Then his world shattered. He rocked back on the chair, almost losing balance, whilst he took in what he had just heard: "Those people back in Plymouth. You know Neil, Robbie and the others in that firm you were working for. I must inform you they were all undercover police officers. Furthermore, they recorded your many conversations with them."

Fulton rocked forward, regaining his balance, then held his head in his hands. Once more, he started to blubber, but only for a moment. He quickly gathered himself and started to put his defence on tape – for the sake of the record.

"I mean, I thought I'd got in with a big firm in England and I just wanted to make myself more important, make myself seen that I was a big man," Jim Fulton said.

"A firm as in gangsters?" asked a detective.

"Right. So, I wanted to make myself out to be a big man."

"Right and so you decided what?"

"Just waffle."

A firm as in gangsters? the interviewer asked. I ask you to remember that word – 'firm' – because this is a true story about the firm that wasn't a firm at all.

Just like Jim Carrey's character in *The Truman Show,* Fulton's environment had been controlled and his life manipulated. He believed he'd been living cheek by jowl in the company of gangsters in Plymouth, England from 1999 to 2001. In fact, he'd been living in a bubble not of his own creation.

The rest of the cast in the 'firm' playing the parts of members of an organised crime group (OCG) are real enough but not genuine. They are all skilled undercover detectives and part of Operation George. This extraordinarily successful police operation was set up in the wake of the murder of the prominent human rights solicitor Rosemary Nelson in Lurgan, Northern Ireland in 1999, and therein lies the catalyst for what came later.

The Nelson Family Home

Monday 15 March 1999 was like any other day. The only anomaly was that Rosemary Nelson slept a little later than usual as she was feeling under the weather, partly because of how she was feeling and also because two of her children were away on a school holiday in France.

It was late morning when her friend, confidante and sec-retary Nuala McCann called by to find her friend still getting ready for work. They planned to have a coffee before travelling in separate cars to the law firm's office a short distance away in Lurgan town centre.

Based on the known facts, it's easy to imagine this is what happened that morning. Letting herself in with a key entrusted to her, Nuala called upstairs, "I'm here, are you ready?"

"I'll be down soon but can you do me a favour?"

"No problem. What is it?"

"Get the *Irish Times*, please. I want to read the Drumcree article and see if they published my picture."

Exchange over, Nuala went to a local newsagent to buy the paper. On her return, both women sat in the kitchen and over coffee briefly chatted about the article and their amusement at Rosemary's picture. "They never use a flattering photo, have you noticed?" Rosemary said and both women laughed.

Nuala drove to the end of a nearby road, expecting to see Rosemary driving her silver BMW past on Lake Street. Confused as to why Rosemary hadn't passed her, Nuala drove around looking for her friend, until she came around a corner to a scene of devastation. Rosemary's BMW was a mass of twisted metal, the work of a terrorist bomb. Nuala rushed to the driver's seat. Her friend was covered in black dust and seemed gravely injured.

Nuala ran to a neighbour's house and asked her to call 999. On returning to her friend, Nuala found another neighbour, a qualified nurse, had arrived. The nurse had heard the explosion and ran to the scene. A short time later a local doctor arrived, followed by an ambulance, paramedics, the fire service, and the police. It should come as no surprise, owing to both her legs having been blown off by the blast, that medics struggled to stabilise Rosemary Nelson or relieve her pain. By the time she was cut her free from the car and taken to Craigavon Hospital there was no more to be done to save her life. Rosemary Nelson died shortly after three o'clock that afternoon.

Later that same day, the Red Hand Defenders, a splinter Loyalist paramilitary group who some claimed was a front for the LVF, claimed responsibility for the bomb in a telephone call to the BBC Newsroom in Belfast.

This gruesome murder was a catalyst in bringing Fulton to justice for other crimes. Though there is no evidence Jim Fulton was implicated in the murder of Rosemary Nelson, he was one of many suspected who had connections to Loyalist paramilitary groups. It was her murder that acted as a mechanism for bringing him and Muriel Gibson to justice for other terrorist crimes including the murders of innocent Catholics and RUC police officers. Fulton was a Nelson murder suspect, but there is no evidence implicating him at all, even to this day.

Soon after Rosemary Nelson's death, both Fulton and Gibson

fled Northern Ireland; Fulton flying to California and Gibson relocating to the West Country in England. Fulton thought he was safe. What he didn't know was that he would soon come to the notice of American law enforcement, including the FBI.

California Dreaming

Murrieta is a township in Riverside County, about eighty miles south of downtown Los Angeles. Nearby Temecula is known for its wine trail and is one of the many attractions in this region of Southern California.

Muriel Gibson had connections to Murrieta. Her former husband, William Landry, and their children lived there in a battered looking yellow house. In September 1999, Jim Fulton flew to the United States then took refuge in that house together with his wife, Tanya, no doubt waiting for the hullaballoo to die down back in Belfast. But Fulton's attempts to lie low were undermined when Tanya discharged a loaded weapon in the grounds of the house. The shots rang out and were heard by some nearby brickyard workers who instinctively ducked for cover. The two workers, Johnny Buckles and Nathan Rouse, were stacking bricks with a forklift truck. Buckles later said, "Two or three shots went off. Then the fourth or fifth went zipping by us a little closer." Rouse claimed they had heard at least a dozen shots. The workers reported the shots to Murrieta police.

Local law enforcement officers arrived to find the Fultons and three other adults at the home. Inside, they found two rifles, expended cartridges, ammunition, and a gun on a shelf. They also seized a .32-caliber handgun and a black T-shirt emblazoned with the slogan "Loyalist Volunteers lead the way."

A news article said, "Police reported finding a number of .22 calibre rifles, an M-72 "spent" anti-tank rocket launcher, a six-inch cannon, mounted on a wooden base, two inert pipe bombs, hollowed out hand grenades with some gun powder residue, as well as 5.5 ounces of hashish and a small amount of methamphetamine."

It continued: "Police said a 33-year-old Las Vegas woman and 29-year-old Tanya Fulton admitted to having fired a handgun out a rear window of the home. Tanya Fulton's lawyer said the shooting erupted after the Las Vegas woman told his client it is legal to own firearms in the United States. The lawyer added, 'Tanya had never fired a gun, and she was told there was a big open field there and apparently a couple of shots were fired out of the window.'"

The Murrieta Sheriff's Department arrested the Las Vegas woman, William James (Jim) and Tanya Fulton, as well as residents Odysseus Landry, 29, and Mahatma Landry, 28, on child-endangerment, drug, and weapon charges. The child endangerment charges were levelled at Jim and Tanya Fulton owing to the presence of their two young children at the house in Murrieta. The children were taken into protective care and were returned to Northern Ireland after their parents were arrested.

The arrests took place on the 16th of December 1999, just nine months after the bomb explosion that killed Rosemary Nelson. Local law enforcement authorities in the town were notified by the FBI to put major security around Fulton almost immediately after they arrested him but were not told the reason. Many questions then started to flow about Fulton and his presence in the United States.

The US press, alerted by reports in Ireland, became aware of the implications of the case. A nationwide TV network referred to Fulton and those arrested with him as a "cell of a dangerous, international Irish terrorist organization." Following that, the Californian arresting officer told the media he had not been approached by the RUC but confirmed police reports from Belfast giving details of prior convictions and other background material on the five people arrested had finally been sent to the US.

On Fulton's appearance at a court remand hearing, the District Attorney told the court the $100,000 bail being asked for each defendant was higher than the normal $5,000 per defendant in such a drug case, but he declined to say why. Jail officials later said, "Regardless of whether Fulton can make bail, the immigration hold will bar his release."

Fulton's California arrest caused quite a commotion at that week's official State Department briefing for journalists at the White House in Washington, with one journalist asking, "What do you know about the arrest last month of a man in Southern California who is suspected of having planted a car bomb that killed Rosemary Nelson in Northern Ireland?"

The terse answer from spokesman James Rubin was, "Yeah, that sounds to me like a domestic law enforcement matter, and I would refer you to the law enforcement agencies."

The same article also reported that "the Assistant Chief Constable of Norfolk Constabulary, Colin Port, who's heading the investigation into Nelson's murder in last year's March 15th car bombing, however, told [us] on Sunday last week that he was aware of the arrest, but had no plans to interview Fulton."

Richard Harvey, a New York-based lawyer, of the Rosemary

Nelson Campaign also started asking how Fulton came to be in possession of an arsenal of weapons, including explosives, and why all charges, except possession of drugs, were dramatically dropped that week. He also asked how Fulton got entry into the US and why he could remain on in contravention of immigration law. All this was going on in the background as United States Congress was holding hearings to bring pressure on the British government to hold an independent inquiry into Nelson's murder.

The explosives and weapons charges were eventually dropped, against the wishes of the local district attorney, who was controversially overruled. The district attorney and arresting officer were only informed about Fulton's loyalist connections when phoned by the *Ireland on Sunday* newspaper almost two weeks following the Murrieta arrests.

Colin Port was undoubtedly truthful but possibly disingenuous when telling the press there were no plans to interview Jim Fulton. That point was a long way off. What few people knew was that Colin Port, as head of the investigation into the Rosemary Nelson murder, had already put a covert operation in place once Muriel Gibson had been located in Plymouth, Devon, England, and after the arrest of the Fultons in California, the first phase of Operation George had commenced with the assistance of the FBI who were undoubtedly instrumental in dropping the charges against Fulton. Jim Fulton's California dreaming would soon become his nightmare.

Colin Port

International pressure was building for a thorough and independent inquiry into the horrific murder of Rosemary Nelson.

As early as 17 March 1999, two days after Nelson's car was blown up, a resolution condemned the murder of Rosemary Nelson, which was referred to the US House of Representatives Committee on International Relations. Amongst other things, it referred to "public knowledge that Rosemary Nelson's life was threatened on a number of occasions by the RUC Special Branch... the North's human rights group, the Committee on the Administration of Justice, has called for an independent investigation into Rosemary Nelson's murder and said it would be 'untenable' for the RUC to head the inquiry... the United States should fully support the implementation of the United Nations Special Rapporteur's recommendation for an independent inquiry into the killing of Belfast lawyer Pat Finucane... calls on the United Nations to condemn these bombings and seek an independent investigation apart from the RUC; calls on the United Nations to form an independent inquiry into the harassment by the RUC of human rights lawyers and the killings of Rosemary Nelson and others."

The Good Friday Agreement (GFA), or Belfast Agreement, are two agreements, not one, but almost always referred to in the singular. They were signed on 10 April 1998, designed to end the violence of the Troubles, which had ensued since the late 1960s. It was a major development in the Northern Ireland peace process of the 1990s. Northern Ireland's present devolved system of government is based on the agreement. The agreement also created several institutions between Northern Ireland and the Republic of Ireland, and between the Republic of Ireland and the United Kingdom.

With that in mind, on the day of Rosemary Nelson's murder and recognising the need for an independent element in the murder investigation, Sir Ronnie Flanagan, then RUC Chief Constable, sought assistance from HM Inspectorate of Constabulary and the Director of the Federal Bureau of Investigation. The result was that Colin Port, the Deputy Chief Constable of Norfolk, was appointed to act as Officer in Overall Command (OIOC) of a murder investigation team (MIT) which became the most extensive murder investigation in the history of Northern Ireland.

Colin Port had spent most of his police career investigating crime, initially with the Greater Manchester Police, rising through the ranks from Detective Constable to Detective Superintendent in charge of Crime Operations and later as a Detective Chief Superintendent. He became the Head of the Criminal Investigation Department (CID) with the Warwickshire Constabulary. In 1994 he had been appointed Investigations Coordinator to the UN International Criminal Tribunal for the former Yugoslavia and in the following year Director of Investigations to the UN International Criminal Tribunal in Rwanda. In 1996 he became Head of the Southeast Regional Crime Squad. He then became Deputy Chief Constable of Norfolk. He went to Northern Ireland with a great deal of experience, particularly the targeting of serious and organised crime groups, using informants, surveillance, undercover officers and intrusive techniques.

Port was not the first to suggest that the best hope of developing a case against those suspects named in the early intelligence lay in pursuing a proactive investigation which could include both human and technical surveillance. Port had referred to it as a possibility at a meeting on 26 March 1999, when Kent police officers from England, FBI Special Agent John Guido, and senior RUC Special Branch (SB) officers, discussed 'technical issues and possible opportunities' and held a 'general discussion about intelligence versus evidence difficulties and the need to protect intelligence gathering tactics whilst exploring every opportunity to secure evidence in this very important case'. Owing to internal RUC politics, it was clear the SB had some reservations about such a course.

However, in the latter half of 1999, significant opportunities arose which enabled the MIT to initiate surveillance without the assistance of SB, using techniques that were less familiar to those targeted and at times and in places when they were almost certainly less watchful. These opportunities arose when two of the murder suspects left Northern Ireland. In September 1999 one of them, William James ('Jim') Fulton, travelled to the USA; another, Muriel Gibson, moved from Portadown, initially to Plymouth and later Cornwall in England. When Jim Fulton returned from the USA to Northern Ireland, he was warned that a threat had been made against his life and so he also moved to Cornwall, where he resided temporarily with Muriel Gibson before finding accommodation of his own. From time to time during the following months both Jim Fulton and Muriel Gibson were visited by others whom the Port MIT regarded as suspects involved in Rosemary Nelson's murder.

Port was also familiar with the CHIS – covert human intelligence source – database back in England. It was originally planned to establish a single database containing details of undercover police officers and confidential informants ('snouts', as they were informally known). That idea was scrapped, resulting in a separate database of nationally accredited undercover officers (UCOs). With Gibson's new location in Plymouth and Fulton's return in mind, Port and others started collating a list of experienced Level 1 undercover officers, those with deep infiltration experience. This list contained the details of the undercover officers who would soon form two teams on the covert intelligence operation, code named George.

Printed in Great Britain
by Amazon